DARK DUETS:
Musical Mayhem

BOOKS BY MICHAEL MCCARTY

DARK DUETS:
Musical Mayhem

BY MICHAEL MCCARTY
AND HIS COLLABORATORS

WILDSIDE PRESS

CONTENTS

SOLO: AUTHOR'S INTRODUCTION

Michael McCarty

The theme of *Dark Duets* is that of music. Dark twisted tunes with bizarro beats, an undead symphony ending with a crescendo of razor-blade French kisses and mad rhythms that make you bleed.

Dance, it's okay.

Dance-dance-dance at the Masquerade Of Death, if you so desire.

I feel this is a unique collection because there are so many voices—all singing and bringing in their expertise, coloring their song or songs with me and making them stronger compositions in the end.

I'd like to thank each of the great vocalists with whom I shared the spotlight and microphone:

P.D. Cacek

Sandra DeLuca

R.L. Fox

Cristopher Hennessey-DeRose

Cindy Hulting

Charlee Jacob

Teri Jacobs
Mark McLaughlin
Michael Romkey
Jeffrey Thomas

Without these singers, I'd only be a solo act. Also, I'd like to thank my family, fans, editors, publishers and various other supporters. Thank you for making sweet music with me over the years including Mom, Dad, Steve, Cathy & David, Carma, Dave & Julie, Scott M, Alan O, Jeff James, Matt & Shocklines, "Hellnotes," Sean Leary, Julie Jensen, Barnes & Noble, Borders, The Edge, Uncle Hugo's, Garrett, The Source, the other Michael McCarty, Julian from Port Of Spain, Scott Edleman, Ron Stewart, A.J. "Dark Krypt," "Filmfax" The Sugar Nipples, The Metrolites.

Bentley Little for writing the insightful introduction to the book. And lastly, John Betancourt for his foresight and support of the genres, Sean Wallace for editing the book and for all the fans for whom without *Dark Duets* would have fallen on deaf ears.

DEDICATION

To Cindy Hulting—
Who always makes my heart sing

Dark Duets is also dedicated to the memories of my favorite
dearly departed singers:

John Lennon
George Harrison
Freddie Mercury
Bon Scott
Elvis Presley
Kurt Cobain
Johnny Cash
Warren Zevon
Billie Holiday
Mama Cass
Buddy Holly
Stevie Ray Vaughan
Johnny Lee Hooker
Janis Joplin
Jim Morrison
Bob Marley
Jimi Hendrix

MICHAEL MCCARTY

Waylon Jennings
Aaliyah
Andy & Maurice Gibb
Michael Hutchence
Frank Sintra
Marvin Gaye
Karen Carpenter

PRELUDE: INTRODUCTION

Bentley Little

I admire writers who can collaborate with other writers—because it's something I could never do. Why? Well, I could give you a song and dance about how art is the expression of an individual sensibility and collaboration just dilutes it, but that's a load of crap. Look at Lennon and McCartney. Or Gilbert and Sullivan. Hell, look at any movie you'd care to name (I don't care how much of an auteurist you are, the fact is that film is the ultimate collaborative medium, with directors, actors, writers, composers, cinematographers and a whole host of other artists all working together to create the finished work).

No, I can't collaborate because of ego. It's as simple as that. I don't want to relinquish control over even the smallest aspect of my work, and the idea of participating in the sort of give-and-take required to meld two distinct voices into one fills me with dread and makes me contemplate serious acts of mayhem.

Michael McCarty has no such hang-ups.

Perhaps his years of interviewing have paved the way for this willingness to work with others. After all, he's spent a lot of time asking authors questions and then shaping their answers into nonfiction articles that illuminate the author's attitudes and beliefs while simultaneously masking his own thoughts and opinions. Or perhaps it's his musical background. He's played as part of a duo and is used to combining disparate instruments to achieve a single unified sound.

I don't know.

All I know is that you hold in your hand a collection of short fiction Michael has written with other genre writers over the past few years. It's an impressive achievement, this cooperative effort, and Michael's ability to adapt to the varied sensibilities of different authors has resulted in stories that are remarkably seamless as well as refreshingly diverse. Indeed, *Dark Duets* features a wide variety of styles and subject matter, from the Laymonesque "Carnie-Vore," a collaboration with P.D. Cacek, to the humorous fantasy of "Super-Clean," written with Cristopher Hennessey-DeRose, to "Skull Job," a dark sexual horror story co-written by Teri Jacobs that would not be out of place in one of the *Hot Blood* books. In a world dominated by theme anthologies and single-author collections filled with interrelated tales, this sort of far-ranging fictional assortment is a welcome addition to the literary landscape.

Ultimately, though, it's not the *way* in which these stories were written that's important. It's not even *who* his cowriters are. It's the fact that the stories themselves are scary and funny and entertaining and provocative: everything that fiction should be.

Like I said, I could never participate in a project like *Dark Duets*.

But I'm very glad that Michael McCarty has.

Mike: *Mark McLaughlin and I are both big fans of VH-1's "Behind The Music." We both love the hilarious satire rockumentary, "This Is Spinal Tap" (who doesn't love the rocking "Big Bottoms"?). I was also heavily influenced by Mark's parody of The Beatles, "When We Was Flab," one of my favorite stories of his. I also drew on some of my experiences of playing in bands. And I tapped into my memories of the days when I was a managing editor for OIL: The Music Magazine—during my tour of duty, I interviewed rock groups and reviewed CDs. I enjoyed writing from the different points-of-view to tell this wicked story with a beat.*

Mark: *Horror and rock 'n' roll work well together. Both of them are about wild extremes of human existence, and lives that have spun out of control. It's hard enough to keep a normal life in control, so there's no telling what the excesses of a superstar lifestyle can do to a person. Just look at the careers of Elvis Presley, Janis Joplin—or even Michael Jackson, for that matter. Fame changes a person—especially in this story, where there's a diabolical supernatural presence lurking in the wings, waiting to take advantage of any opportunity to thrive.*

SEX, DRUGS & ROT 'N' ROLL

Michael McCarty and Mark McLaughlin

When rock 'n' roll goes the way of the dinosaurs, musicologists of the future may find it hard to believe such an outlandish species of sound ever existed. They also may have difficult comprehending the success of some of the high-concept—or more often, no-concept—groups that managed to scale the dizzying heights of the pop charts. Certainly the heavy-metal/industrial-hardcore/glam-goth group Meat Wagon will seem like some kind of dubious fabled beast, made up by bored rock journalists.

But Meat Wagon was real—as real as the stench that assails your nostrils when you open the corrugated-iron door of a tool shed during a summer heatwave and discover a corpse that's been left to stew and brew for three weeks.

Here is the complete story of the band Meat Wagon, as told by the ones best qualified to tell it: the Meat Wagon gang. Here you will find shocking yet illuminating excerpts from various interviews with Critter, Metalhead, Gothik Gustave and The Lady In Black. Also interwoven are recollections from those who knew them: their manager Fever Dawg, Sir Walter Buckingham of Badbone Productions, the band's spokesman Derek Silverstein, and rock 'n' roll historian Dan Swamp, who also served for fifteen years as editor of *Slag Magazine*.

Meat Wagon's rocket ride to superstardom was fueled by drugs, rage, lust, dark worship—and guuku juice. So buckle yourself in and turn up the volume. This is the story of one of the loudest, most outrageous and ultimately, blasphemous bands in rock history.

THE BIRTH OF MEAT WAGON

There are several rumors circulating about the origins of Meat Wagon. Some people believe that Critter and Metalhead were paternal twins, born backstage at Woodstock. Others claim that The Lady In Black prolonged her life for decades with daily goat-placenta injections, and all the other band members were her children. But what is the truth?

Critter, Metalhead, Gothik Gustave and The Lady In Black. Their real names were, respectively, Anthony Sweet, Dean Greenberg, Gus Martin and Hilda Lawrence—but they left those names behind years ago.

Anthony Sweet was born with vertical pupils and a slight harelip, giving his lean face a startling, catlike appearance. Dean Greenberg's parents died in a car crash a week after his birth, and he was raised by an abusive grandmother who was also a conceptual artist and self-styled witch. He took to wearing home-made masks in his late teens—first white half-masks, reminiscent of the Phantom of the Opera, then later, metal masks that covered most of his head. Gus Martin stopped growing when he hit three feet tall. Hilda Lawrence loved eating paste as a child, and she never outgrew that desire to ingest unnatural substances. In the everyday world, those four were simply misfits — but when they entered the realm of rock 'n' roll, they became living legends.

Here is the real story of the origins of the group, which was formed in 1983:

Critter: I used to play lead guitar with this pathetic cover band called Stardust Ballet. We did all the Top 40 tunes of the time — songs by Culture Club, Huey Lewis And The News, Naked Eyes, Thomas Dolby, Men At Work, a few others. At performances, they made me wear sunglasses so my eyes wouldn't freak people out. Do you know how boring it is to play guitar for synthesizer-heavy pop crap? About as enjoyable as masturbating with that Freddy Krueger claw.

Gothik Gustave: For a long time, I traveled with the circus. There isn't much work in the music industry for someone who's only three feet tall. I used to be Professor Micro-Mite, out there in the midway sideshow with Bearded Betty and the Incredible Gator Boy. I loved singing so I tried out for several bands to get out of the carnival business. Every band I auditioned for would say, "Dude, you have a great voice — but you have to be 'this high' to be our leader singer."

Dan Swamp: Gothik Gustave had to be the shortest person in heavy metal — but he had the tallest voice. Really, his voice was somewhere around eight feet tall. I have an ear for height.

Metalhead: During the late '70s, I was into metal. Steel construction, that is. I worked construction sites, pounding out my frustration with a jackhammer. My life was going nowhere. Crummy past, shitty present, no foreseeable future — I hated this dirty fuckhole of a planet. I was filled with rage and it had to come out somehow. I had to beat something. Eventually I picked up playing the drums, and that did the trick — and paid some bills, too.

The Lady In Black: That was back when I was a crackwhore. The only instrument I played back then was the skin flute, in alleys, flea-bag motels and more backseats than I care to remember. I did every nasty thing imaginable to score crack cocaine. One of my johns didn't have any cash, so he gave me an old bass guitar. It was easy to learn. It only had four stupid strings.

Sir Walter Buckingham: The '70s? The '80s? Hell, I'm in my nineties. Come back later. It's time for my nap.

Fever Dawg: Back then, I was working for my family's funeral business. I lived above the funeral parlor—I could look down into the Grief Grotto from my bathroom window. I drove the hearse, too. I even took my girlfriend on dates in it. She didn't like to make out in the back, but that's life in the death industry. That hearse always had some stiff meat riding in it.

Derek Silverstein: I was in college during that time, studying to be an English major. I read Shakespeare, Hemingway, Twain—all those literary dead guys. I crammed in those classics between smoking home-made bongs and getting drunk until I puked—until one day, out of the blue, I'd earned my sheepskin and had to go out and get a job.

Critter: I was bored out of my gourd with Stardust Ballet, so I used to go to different bars around Chicago and sit in on their open mike nights. There was a club on Lincoln that used to be called Skulls & Crossbones—now it's a furniture store. I was playing my guitar, just wailing it—I played so loud there were ears bleeding in the audience. After that particular show, this ugly dwarf waddled up to me and said he wanted to buy me a drink. I told him I wasn't gay and even if I were, I wouldn't do it with a runt. He just laughed and bought me a drink anyway. And when he laughed—man, that tongue of his just flapped out of his mouth and started waggling in the air. It made him look like a bullfrog, fishing the air for flies. It really creeped me out—I couldn't believe it was real.

Gothik Gustave: It's my tongue. Mine, all mine—every inch of it. Wanna yank on it for proof?

Dan Swamp: Gothik Gustave had the longest tongue in rock 'n' roll. Some believe he had an anteater's tongue grafted into his mouth to achieve that effect. I think, though, that his tongue was too thick for an anteater, which has a narrow, almost tube-like snout. His would have choked an anteater, I think.

Critter: This tiny dude said he worked for the circus and was dying to do some music. Most of the customers had left Skull & Crossbones by then. I was completely drunk, so I picked up my guitar and started playing some crazy made-up shit. And the little guy started singing some mumbo-jumbo just as loud as my guitar. Beer glasses started busting. Mirror were cracking. Outside, a pane in a telephone booth exploded—windshields of cars in the parking lot imploded. It was amazing. I asked him what his name was and he said, "Gothik Gustave." Now I call him G.G. for short.

Gothik Gustave: It was really an off-night for me. I was getting over a cold, so I couldn't hit some of the high notes—my throat had some phlegm in it. And because Critter was just making shit up on the spot, I had to, just to show him I could. I didn't have any real lyrics. I just sang the names of all the constellations and planets I could think of, since his guitar reminded me of rocket engines.

Dan Swamp: That guitar and vocal improvisation was the foundation for "Starman Manstar," a song from the group's debut CD, *Ride The Meat Wagon*.

Sir Walter Buckingham: The first time I heard "Starman Manstar," I thought—how odd, the lyrics sound like an astronomy lesson. And, there wasn't a chorus. The song stretched out over seven minutes. I had no idea how to edit it, so I just faded it out during the last guitar solo. It got a lot of airplay on college radio, which really surprised me.

Critter: I was tired of playing lame covers and was thinking of forming a new band, so I asked G.G. if he wanted to join my group. The little man was totally down with that.

Gothik Gustave: I was psyched! I asked Critter if he wanted to party and he said, "Hell, yeah!"

Critter: We hit a few more bars, and as we were staggering down the street, I decided I was going to find a woman for G.G.

Gothik Gustave: Because I'm so incredibly short and ugly, I usually don't attract the attention of women, unless maybe they're mentally ill or deformed. But Critter's wallet was fat, so finding me some action wasn't too much of a problem. Soon we found this gal wearing a black dress, black stocking, shoes, black everything. Even black lipstick.

The Lady In Black: I saw this drunk guy with funny eyes and a dwarf stumbling around, and they asked if I'd give the little guy a BJ. They were carrying a guitar, so I told them, "Okay, but I only do cash, no musical instruments. That's how I got stuck with a four-string guitar—it was so boring to play, I learned the damn thing in two hours."

Critter: I said, "You mean—a bass guitar?" And she said, "Yeah, that thing." So I told her, "After you're finished with Gustave, we could give you an audition for a band we're forming." She was so happy she gave us a discount on her services.

Gothik Gustave: Everybody thinks I have an incredible tongue—it doesn't even compare to The Lady In Black's.

Critter: We went back to her pad, two floors up from a Mexican restaurant. The Lady In Black took G.G. into the bathroom and did the deed. I thought it was kind of funny she didn't want to use the bedroom, but I didn't want to pry into this gal's personal life. After they were done, we decided to jam on "Starman Manstar" again, with The Lady In Black on bass. G.G.'s vocals were so incredible, my balls swelled.

The Lady In Black: The guys didn't know that my boyfriend Metalhead was sleeping in the next room. Metalhead was okay with my life as a crackwhore—to him, that was an acceptable career. I once talked about going to secretarial school and that sent him into a rage.

Usually he can sleep through anything—but "Starman Manstar" woke him up.

Metalhead: It sounded cool. I was still a little sleepy when I walked in on them. I was wearing only boxer shorts, so I think it freaked the two guys out.

Critter: We stopped playing. I mean, when you see a guy coming toward you who's nearly seven feet tall—with a metal mask, wearing only boxers with his pecker hanging out . . . What can I say? It was distracting.

Gothik Gustave: I thought he was going to kill us. But instead, he stumbled back into his room, dragged out some drums and said, "Back to the top! One, two, three—"

Critter: I've played with a lot of drummers in my life, but I never heard anyone pound the living shit out of the skins like that before. I felt the vibrations all the way through my spine. We had to let him in the band. He could have ripped off our limbs as easily as a snotty-nosed kid tearing the legs off a grasshopper.

The Lady In Black: I was so happy to be part of the band, I let all the guys drink some of my guuku juice. It's bright orange—kind of pretty. The main ingredients come from dead jellyfish, rotten skins from certain exotic toads, and some stuff squeezed out of the carcasses of jumbo tree spiders. Most alcohol is made from fermented plant juices, right? Well, this stuff's made from the decayed tissues and glands of venomous creatures. It's some strong toxic shit—it'll give you some amazing visions. It has to be mixed with a whole lot of pineapple juice, so that it tastes good and doesn't kill ya. I bought it from a crazy old lady who lived three blocks away. She came from the island of Pokaluhu—that's also where Metalhead's grandma was born. Folks there drink guuku juice like us Americans drink pop. They can't get enough of it.

FAQ:

Q: Where did you get the name Meat Wagon?

Metalhead: We eventually met Fever Dawg, and he fell in love with our music and became our manager. He even moved us into the space above his family's funeral home. He lived right there with us. He even hauled our equipment in his hearse.

Fever Dawg: A midnight-blue 1973 Cadillac hearse.

Metalhead: We gave the hearse the nickname "Meat Wagon." Whenever any of us had to drive around on errands, we'd say, "Time to ride the Meat Wagon!" The band's original name was Black Death Sex Machine, but eventually we decided that Meat Wagon would play better in the Midwest. People in the Midwest eat a lot of pork and beef.

Q: How did you get signed to Badbone Productions?

Critter: We were playing out on the road for about a year, going from one shithole bar to the next. We sold tapes out of the back of the hearse and by mail order. The money barely covered our gas and groceries. Then this teenage kid from England sent a fan letter to our P.O. box, saying an American friend had given him one of our tapes, and he wanted us to play his fourteenth birthday party. The kid was Elliott Buckingham and his father was Sir Walter Buckingham, a famous producer and owner of Badbone Productions.

The brat's dad paid for a plane ticket and set us up in the sixteenth-century castle where he lived. We joined Badbone Productions the very next day—because Elliott was turning blue, holding his breath until his dad signed us.

David Silverstein: Sir Walter put me on the case with Meat Wagon right after he signed them. He said, "This band—they're going to be nothing but trouble. Keep an eye on them." He didn't mind trouble, though—not really. Trouble can mean big money sometimes. People want their rock stars to be bad-asses. The hornier and crazier, the better. And there was nobody hornier or crazier than the Meat Wagon gang.

Q: What is your favorite Meat Wagon song?

Gothik Gustave: "Zombie Insomniacs."

Critter: "Bay At The Moon."

The Lady In Black: "Orange Demon In My Brain."

Metalhead: "Rattle Them Bones."

Fever Dawg: "Underground Dwellings."

Sir Walter Buckingham: (He was napping at this point in the interview.)

Derek Silverstein: I lost my virginity while listening to "Basketcase" so I would have to say, that one.

Dan Swamp: "Zombie Insomniacs" had a great sense of raw power. The lyrics—well, they combined some pretty standard goth and heavy-metal themes, and the rhyme was a little off, but still, there was something more . . . A sense of conviction, I think. I would be listening to that one, and I'd say to myself, "I bet they believe all that." Sometimes I even found myself believing.

SAMPLE LYRICS:

"Zombie Insomniacs"
(lyrics by The Lady In Black and Gothik Gustave):

Sleep no more! You'd better stay up.
Squealing demons dig their way up—
right into your plastic-covered tacky living room.
No escape, they will defeat you,
scratch and claw and bite and eat you—
sink into the lava as the Devil seals your doom!

(Chorus)
From their graves the corpses creep—
Hell's so loud, they just can't sleep.
Earth shall not recover from the deadly attacks
of those ass-stinking, guuku-drinking
Zombie Insomniacs!

Daddy never loved me. Mommy was a whore.
Granny took her teeth out to give blowjobs door-to-door.
Life is just a rusty bucket filled with feces and lies!
All you ever think about is murder and sin.
Death is coming for you with a shit-eating grin.
Your corpse will make a midnight snack for maggots and flies!

(Repeat Chorus)

The Lady In Black: There were two versions of "Zombie Insomniacs." In the radio version, "ass-stinking" was replaced with "orange-eyed" and "feces" became "cobwebs." "Whore" went to "bore," "blowjobs" became "kisses" and "shit-eating" turned into "maniac."

Gothik Gustave was pissed off, but I didn't mind. I mean, little kids listen to the radio. Kids should stay innocent as long as possible. Time and disappointment will harden them up eventually.

THE HISTORY OF MEAT WAGON IN ONE-HUNDRED WORDS OR LESS:

Dan Swamp: I'm suppose to sum up the entire history of Meat Wagon in one-hundred words? Or less? It took me over six-hundred pages in my official history of the band, entitled *Guuku Juice On Their Lips: The Complete History Of Meat Wagon.* Well, here goes:

The heavy-metal/industrial-hardcore/glam-goth group Meat Wagon was composed of the four most dysfunctional creatures that ever walked upright—Critter, Metalhead, Gothik Gustave and The Lady In Black. They scored twenty hit singles, with seven reaching No. 1. They recorded fifteen platinum CDs, eighteen gold, and "Rattle Them Bones" stayed on the charts for a record forty-two weeks. They starred in the horror movie, *Dawn of the Zombie Insomniacs,* and were featured in the guuku juice documentary, *Swim the Orange River.* They were gods—or devils. In rock, there's not much difference between the two.

MEAT WAGON ON THE SILVER SCREEN:

Metalhead: My grandmother Vupoggi was from the tropical island of Pokaluhu. Life is pretty different there. They have hotels, tourist attractions and all that, and yet cannibalism is legal. Most of the native people worship an octopus god called Kugappa. We filmed most of *Dawn of the Zombie Insomniacs* on Pokaluhu, and that was fun—it was like a paid vacation, working on a beautiful island. A lot of folks have commented on how realistic the zombie attack scenes look. You'd think those zombies were really tearing into their victims, ripping them up and eating them. Great special effects? Well, let me put it this way. The extras who played the zombies were all natives of Pokaluhu. And the folks playing the victims—well, there was no need to pay any of them after shooting was done.

Gothik Gustave: Yeah, a pile of bones can't cash a check!

Derek Silverstein: *Dawn of the Zombie Insomniacs* was a publicity nightmare. Once people found out they were watching actual scenes of cannibalism—the church groups all went nuts. And ticket sales went through the roof. Album sales, too. In America, the number of cannibalism-related crimes went up about three-hundred percent. In Europe, they went up seven-hundred percent, which I thought was pretty interesting. The beef in Europe isn't very good—it's so stringy. Maybe that movie gave some people ideas.

Critter: The natives all thought I was some kind of sacred guy because of my eyes. They called me 'He Who Opens The Way'—that was pretty cool. They even held a luau in my honor. They wanted to wrap G.G. in palm leaves and cook him up, but I talked them out of it.

The Lady In Black: Over the years, I've tried pretty much every chemical associated with expanding the boundaries of the human mind, and that trip to Pokaluhu really got me thinking. That whole 'opening the way' concept seemed so intriguing. I talked with some of the holy women on the island, and they explained that 'the way' was in fact the threshold between this dimension and that of the gods. Their top deity was Kugappa, and they said that while he can manifest a physical body on this plane, his actual soul resides somewhere *out there*. Wouldn't it be fantastic to visit the dimension of the gods? Wouldn't that be the ultimate trip?

Guuku juice is legendary for having the ability to expand one's perceptions. I did some more research on the stuff, since I wanted to see if it could be used as part of that whole 'opening the way' concept. I mean, I actually know 'He Who Opens The Way'—though we call him Critter, ha!—so I figured, maybe we could get that way opened up somehow. Eventually I got involved in that documentary, *Swim the Orange River*. All of us appeared in that—we played victims of the Inquisition in some dramatic reenactments. I guess Torquemada drank an obscure European

23

version of guuku juice all the time. Even after the documentary was finished, we all stayed in touch with the folks who produced it—the Order of the Orange Dawn. A lot of rich, influential folks are involved with that order. Guuku juice is pretty powerful stuff—in more ways than one.

MORE SAMPLE LYRICS:

"Orange Demon In My Brain"
(lyrics by The Lady In Black and Critter):

Secrets inked on ancient vellum—
terror in my cerebellum—
If you see the Devil, tell 'em
something has escaped from Hell
and lives inside my head!
Somehow it has cast a spell
to make my brain undead!
(Chorus)
Orange demon in my brain—
he calls to me!
Orange demon shall remain—
he crawls to me!
All I do is think about him.
I could never live without him!

Now I have a brain of madness—
never more shall I know sadness—
evil fills my soul with gladness!
Fantasies of orange fire
make the world seem dead and dull!
Wicked visions of desire
lurk within my haunted skull!

(Repeat Chorus)

THE JONESTOWN ANNIVERSARY CONCERT:

Fever Dawg: After twenty years of fame and fortune, wealth and glory, heavy MTV rotation and enough sex, drugs and rock 'n' roll to kill twelve teen garage bands, Meat Wagon decided to leave this dimension and try another.

For their twentieth anniversary, the group wanted to hold an outdoor concert at Jonestown in the country of Guyana in South America, the place where over nine-hundred people committed suicide by drinking poisoned Kool-Aid. This time, Meat Wagon wanted everyone to drink guuku juice. Not only would it open the audience's senses to new perceptions, but it would also open the gateway to another dimension.

Sir Walter Buckingham: Guuku juice? I have a little swig out of my flask every now and then. The Lady In Black hooked me on the stuff. I think it's the only thing keeping me alive. At my age, it makes me so sleepy. But I have some really fabulous dreams. Lovely . . . (So saying, Sir Walter fell asleep.)

Derek Silverstein: I told the gang, "What are you thinking? This gig will never fly! It's too bizarre! Too scary!" But they wouldn't listen. At that point, they were hanging out a lot with cult members from the Order of the Orange Dawn. I never knew who any of the cultists were, since they all wore hats with veils — even the men. Fedoras with orange lace hanging over the face. What's up with that? Metalhead even painted his masks orange, and The Lady In Black started wearing orange accessories.

Dan Swamp: The Order of the Orange Dawn helped to supply them with enough guuku juice for the event. I went to that concert, as did every rock journalist in the world. Folks wanted to know: What the Hell is this? Why hold a concert in Guyana? People were expecting a weird-ass scene, and in that regard, nobody was disappointed.

Fever Dawg: I guess they held it in Guyana because, as The Lady In Black told me, the place still had a lot of psychic energy hovering around. Some places have more energy than others, and I guess that place was a regular powerhouse. Who knows, maybe that used to be the site of an ancient temple or something. The universe is full of crazy shit, and we don't know the half of it. We don't know a tenth, not even a hundredth of it.

Derek Silverstein: I quit the day before the Guyana concert. I mean, they weren't listening to me, and I didn't want to be the one to talk to the press if the whole gig went straight to Hell. These days I work for a boy band out of Rio de Janeiro.

Dan Swamp: It was amazing. The crowd was absolutely humungous. There were dozens of refreshment stands, staffed by members of the Order of the Orange Dawn. They had guuku juice straight-up, guuku juice slushies, various guuku-based cocktails—I ordered the slushy, and really, it was pretty good. Especially since it was such a scorcher of a day. I tried not to think of all that dead crap guuku juice is actually made of.

The band came out amidst thunderous applause and immediately launched into "Starman Manstar." From there they went to "Zombie Insomniacs" and "Rattle Them Bones." I remember thinking: we're all drinking this freaky guuku juice, so maybe they should call it rot 'n' roll. Yeah. The heart of rot 'n' roll is still beating. It's only rot 'n' roll, but I like it.

Then they played "Orange Demon In My Brain" and a lot of folks in the audience joined in—but they weren't singing the song. They were singing something very rhythmic, very fierce— I couldn't make out the words, but as I listened, I realized that they were actually chanting in a sing-song sort of way, and the name "Kugappa" was repeated regularly.

By that time, I was sucking down my fourth slushy, and the combination of the guuku juice, the music, the heat, the chanting—I could feel it all taking hold of me. Then Critter suddenly began to gesture toward the skies. He moved his arms round and round above his head, like he was stirring something. And he was.

Stirring up trouble.

The air above the stage began to ripple like water—concentric, shining circles, pulsing outward, over and over. I wasn't the only one to see it. Hundreds of others were pointing up into the sky.

Suddenly the circles began to change, turning bluish-pink, then pinkish-red, then finally bright orange.

Next came the tentacles.

They were everywhere, pouring down from out of the ripples, grabbing at audience members and pulling them up into the sky, where they'd disappear from sight. Then a fresh batch of tentacles would come swooping down, grabbing for more. People weren't screaming or anything—they simply continued chanting, spellbound. Soon I found myself chanting. Still, I was lucky—the tentacles didn't get me. But they did get the band.

I think that's what the Meat Wagon gang wanted, because they kept singing as they were being carried up, up and away. And the minute the music stopped, the tentacles and the ripples in the sky all faded away. Folks stopped chanting and looked around, completely dazed. They slowly began to realize what had just happened.

That's when the screaming started.

Sir Walter Buckingham: (Waking up) Oh, hello. You're still here?

I just had the most beautiful dream. The Lady In Black and all the boys were in it. Even the tiny one, Gothik Gary, Augustus, whatever his name was. I was walking on a beach with sand as white as snow. To my right was the sea. I saw the Meat Wagon gang playing in the water. Then they saw me and began to swim toward me. They still had human heads, but the rest of them–! The Lady In Black had a body like a spider, covered with slimy scales. Critter had clusters of tentacles instead of arms, and Metalhead had flippers, tendrils like a jellyfish and a mouthful of horrible teeth. The little one had warty toad-skin and crab pincers, too—and he was laughing, wagging that horrible tongue of his.

"Oh, dear," I said, "none of you can play your instruments any more."

They looked at each other, smiled, and then they all turned toward me. They opened their mouths and the most incredible sounds came out. Chattering, chirping, squealing, cheeping, roaring—deep-sea sounds, the sort made by whales and dolphins and other ocean creatures. In rhythm! It was quite compelling. Hypnotic. Beautiful. Certainly no need for any instruments. I could have listened to it for days. But then I woke up.

Now where did I put that flask? Ah, here it is. Time for a little nip.

If you'll excuse me, I'm going back to sleep. I want to see if I can catch the rest of that song.

Mike: *I wanted to collaborate with P.D. Cacek ever since I read her brilliant bloodsucker novel,* Night Prayer. *I met Trish at the World Horror Convention in Denver in 2000. I interviewed her shortly after the con for* Giants Of The Genre. *After the interview we corresponded each other with several funny e-mails and phone calls. During one of those conversations, I jokingly suggested after Canyons came out, we should collaborate on a werewolf story. As they say, the rest is history.*

One of the characters of the story, Tommy Wharton, returns in another story called "From The Bowels Of The Earth" (this time co-written with Mark McLaughlin).

Trish: *A collaboration is a very strange creature — it can be conceived without its parents realizing what they've done. A word here, an idea there, or, in the case of "Carnie-Vore" the continuation of a theme and a new "life" is created. I'm proud to be the 'mama.'*

CARNIE-VORE

Michael McCarty & P.D. Cacek

The carnival was a bust.

Worse than a bust, it was lame...and that said it all.

Every year the Mid-American Carnival had been the high point of summer vacation. For months, every teen within a twenty-mile radius would survive the hot, sticky days anticipating what new "Freaks" (a.k.a. "The Anamorphically Challenged," if you wanted to be Political Correct about the whole thing) the carnival had found to go with the old stand-bys: the Headless Woman, the Mutant Babies, and Stan, Stan, The Reptilian Man.

Every year . . . except this one.

This year nothing went right. A carney worker dropped the Headless Woman's special-effect mirror, thereby destroying the "illusion," so she had to sit in the sweltering tent with an ill-fitting black hood over her head. One of the Mutant Babies had been jostled a little too much in transport, and upended—displaying the MATTEL brand on its little plastic rump. And Stan, Stan found a cure for his xeroma and retired from the circuit.

It just wasn't fair. This was suppose to be her year... the year she finally stopped being a baby and became a real-life teenager. This year sucked big time.

"Dammit," Paula Cunningham growled at her reflection in the fly-specked mirror of the Ladies Room. "It's not fair."

"What isn't, girlfriend?" Debbi Kanter asked as she swirled out of the stall like she was stepping onto a dance floor. "Wow, why are you so bummed?"

Paula met her friend's eyes in the glass and signed. Debbi was everything Paula wasn't and wanted to be. A full eighteen months older, Debbi already knew the secrets of being a successful teen—if the rumors around school were true.

Shifting her gaze, Paula looked back at her pouting reflection and felt her budding breasts sag a little beneath the tank-top her mother had selected for that morning. Full lips, blond hair, dark eyes, and enough make-up to cover up the half-dozen angry pimples that decorated her forehead. She was some catch, all right.

"The carnival sucks," she said when she noticed Debbi was waiting for an explanation. "All the rides are lame and the freaks aren't...except for the one I'm with."

Debbi's mirror image reflected pity at her. "Yeah, I wondered about that. So how come you're with Tommy Wharton anyway? I thought your mom grounded you from dating when she caught you toking with Sean?"

Paula licked the pout off the cherry red color on her lips. At least there were rumors about her, too . . . that was something.

"Yeah, she did. But she's been pestering me to go out with him all summer . . . I guess she's making an exception because he's the mayor's son."

"I guess. But shit, Tommy Wharton."

"Yeah." Paula watched Debbi grab the can of extra-super-hold and squirted a cloud of it into her hair. Her own hair was happily frizzing from the humidity. "My mom said she doesn't want me hanging around guys with more meat between their legs than on their bones."

"No way! Your mom really said that?"

"Yeah."

"Shit, your mom's so cool!" Debbi added another layer and tossed her the can, like she knew what to do with it. "Well, then she should love you going out with Tommy. But, shit . . . Tommy Wharton."

"Yeah," Paula said, "I know. He's a pig."

A real pig. Every chance he got since picking her up, he'd try to feel her up. And it only got worse once they got to the carnival. In the Haunted House, he'd squeezed her breasts so hard she knew that if she looked hard enough, she'd be able to see bruises through the top's thin material. In the Maze of Mirrors she'd not only had to see a hundred reflections of him, but a hundred reflections of him with his hands down the front of her shorts. And just the thought of the "promised ride" in the back seat of his father's hand-me-down-Lexus made her want to puke out her guts.

Sometimes she really hated her mother.

"Well," Debbi said, tossing her head, "Tommy's definitely no Don Juan."

"No, he's more like Dom DeLuise."

They laughed and that made the whole situation a little better. A little, but not much.

"Well, keep the faith, girlfriend. He'll be going off to college in a few weeks and you won't have to worry about him for a while."

"Thank God for small favors."

"That's what I hear..." Debbie howled at the joke that went right over Paula's head. "Hey, I heard there's a new monster freak show this year."

All of Paula's carefully maintained depression was on the verge of lifting. "Yeah?"

"Yeah, supposed to be really scary. Only thing is, it starts after dark . . . eight or something like that. Frank and I are going. You should drag Tommy's fat ass in . . . maybe it'll scare the crap out of him. With a load in his pants he might leave you alone."

Paula doubted two broken legs and a ruptured bladder would keep Tommy off her, but smiled hopefully and followed her older and wiser friend out into the bright, clammy sunlight.

Tommy Wharton stood outside the concrete "Comfort Station," sweating and shifting from one foot to the other as he waited for Paula to finish. And it felt like he'd been waiting for an hour.

He once asked his father why women took so long in the john. He figured his dad would know since it seemed his mom spent most of her time locked in the master bath. But his old man only smiled and winked . . . as if he was supposed to know what that meant.

In truth, he couldn't figure that out any more than he could figure out women or their habits. He'd only had two 'real' dates in four years of high school—both ending more prematurely than he'd wanted—and he spent Prom Night at home, eating Ding Dongs and watching "Saturday Night Live" reruns on Nick At Night.

Wiping the sweat away from his eyes. Tommy happened to look down and saw his shadow. If he'd been a ground hog he'd never come out of his hole. He hated being fat, but not enough to stop his daily intake of Ding Dongs and Twinkies. If he'd been given the choice he would have looked like Arnie Schwarzenegger, but he came from a long line of obese politicians. His corpulent great-granddaddy had been an alderman, his chubby grandfather was a former city councilman and his dad was currently the stout mayor. Genetics had predetermined his life as the next generation's spherical public official.

Not that he hadn't tried to fight the congential curse. He'd joined both Weight Watchers and Jenny Craig, did the Oprah diet religiously (only on Sundays), the grapefruit diet until sores appeared in his mouth, the cabbage and yeast diet (a bad idea all around) . . . and the only weight he lost was to his wallet.

It wasn't fair.

But then again, waiting in the hot sun for some preppie bee-och wasn't fair, either. Fat or not, he was the mayor's son and that in itself demanded respect.

Tommy turned sideways as he checked his watch—what was taking her so long?—and noticed his shadow had a boner. One hard enough to cut diamonds. *Shit!* Backing into the bathroom's shadow as quickly as possible, he stuck his hand into his pocket to straighten things out . . . and heard the roar of laughter.

"Hey, look who it is," Joe Campbell, the high school's head jock and line-backer, yelled to his pack of hyenas. "Tubby Wart-Ton. Y'know, Tubby, you're suppose to play with yourself inside the john, not out in public. You wanna scare the kiddies?"

Joe got slapped on his back and High-Five'd from his buddies as if he'd just said something witty.

"Ho, ho." Tommy snarled and was instantly rewarded with another chorus of whoops.

"Shit, Tubby, you gotta practice more if you want to be Santa," Joe smirked. "It's 'ho, ho, HO' asshole."

Sensing defeat, Tommy took his hand out of his pocket and started messing with his hair as he turned around. Paula, pretty little Paula, was standing right there.

Shit, shit, shit.

"What happened?" He asked as he grabbed her arm and began dragging her toward the Cinnabar booth. It made him feel better when he noticed her stumbling. "You fall in?"

"N-n-no . . . I was talking to Debbi. She says there's a way-cool monster show over at the Freak Tent. Wanna go?"

"Hell no."

"Aw, please Tommy. I'd . . . e it, but it's at night and I'd be too scared . . . I need someone big and strong I can hang on to."

"It starts at night?" Tommy's stomach began rumbling when it caught the first scent of hot grease and cinnamon. "No."

Tommy's stomach suddenly dropped in priority when he felt Paula's hand gently brush the front of his pants.

"Oh, please Tommy? It'll be dark and maybe we can . . . you know."

Tommy knew, Christ did he know. Cinnabar forgotten, he lead

her away from the concession area and toward the parking lot. A little preview of coming attractions wasn't out of the question . . . especially since he was going to be nice and shell out hard cash to take her to some dumb-ass freak show. Hell, he deserved a little preview for being such a good guy.

But it was amazing how she could sound like his mom sometimes.

They stood outside a side entrance of the Freak Tent, the floodlight making monsters out of people's shadows. One light had been aimed directly at the hand-drawn poster of a werewolf, crimson blood dripping from yellow fangs and claws, the caption shimmering in the glare: REAL-LIFE WEREWOLF!

Paula shook her head. This, she thought, this was what she let Tommy see her naked for?

Not fair.

A passionless barker stood on an upturned bucket next to the opening, microphone in hand, trying to entice the gawking crowd. "Come one, come all. Come see the real-life werewolf. More frightening than the beast in *An American Werewolf In London* or the one in Paris. More scary than all seven *Howling* movies combined." Yawn. "Show starts in a few minutes. Tickets are going fast, so get yours now."

Paula looked at the werewolf's painted eyes and tugged Tommy's arm. "Let's go inside."

"I don't know," Tommy said, shifting from side to side nervously. "It's probably some flea-bitten mutt or something."

The barker turned and smiled. "Ain't no dog in there, boy. Come on, now, take the little lady to the show." His voice boomed through the speakers. "You ain't scared already, are you?"

"Of a fake werewolf? Hell no," Tommy answered quickly. "Come on." But Paula was already standing next to the barker, dancing lightly on her toes.

"Your little lady's mighty anxious," the man said, winking at her. "That'll be ten bucks, sport."

"What? You've got to be kidding!"

"Nope, a dollar a ticket, and five tickets a piece comes to ten bucks."

"Why so much?"

Paula rolled her eyes. His whining was getting on her nerves.

"Cause, sport, the werewolf can only do one show a night. Can't make a living like the other shows that can perform all day." The barker lowered his mike and leaned in close. "Tell ya what, sport, slip me an extra fiver and I'll make sure you get front row seats. How's that for a bargain?"

When Tommy started to shake his head, Paula pressed up against his body and gave him her sexiest voice.

"Please, Tommy? Plee-ee-ze?"

You would have thought she'd dropped her knees and given his noodle the sucking of its tiny life. Tommy almost tore his pocket getting the money out.

Smiling, Paula forced herself to hold his hand as they followed the barker into the crowded tent and were shown to their seats directly in front of the 'stage' — a raised platform on which stood a large black cage. The man inside that cage had shoulder-length brown hair and wore only a skin-tight pair of jeans and smiled. He winked at Paula, then rolled his shoulders and began pacing, back to front. In a minute, his body was glistening with sweat.

It was impressive.

After a few more minutes, during which Paula fought off Tommy's fumbling, the house lights began to dim . . . and Tommy took the opportunity to slither a hand onto her thigh.

Paula slapped it away loud enough to make the man sitting on her opposite side jump.

"Come on, baby-doll," Tommy pleaded in her ear. "I got us some prime seats didn't I? We're up nice and close to where all the action is, aren't we?"

Shit. She let him get his hand half-way down the front of her shorts before stopping him.

"But the action;s up there." Paula made her giggle, pointing to the cage where the half-naked man had stopped prowling to grip the bars of his cage. "Later, Tommy . . . I promise. Shhh, it's starting."

Nodding to the man in the cage, the barker stepped onto the stage and raised a hand for silence. The audience obeyed in varying degrees.

"Ladies and gentlemen," the barker said into his mike, "you are about to witness the transformation of Warren Trudy . . . the last of a line of creatures known as werewolves. Those of you with weak hearts are advised to leave . . . and leave quickly, for the moon is about to rise."

Nobody left, but there were a few giggles from the darkened tent.

Paula held her breath. Fake or not, she loved this sort of stuff. Warren Trudy, what a bogus name for a werewolf!

"Now, I must warn you, ladies and gentlemen, when Warren transforms, please remain calm. Do not panic. Don't from your seats. He's behind iron bars and can't harm you . . . however, should the unthinkable happen and he somehow manages to break free, he will attack the first thing he sees." The barker paused for dramatic effect. "Quiet, please. The moon has risen."

At that moment all the lights went out and the tent was plunged into darkness. Despite the barker's warning to be quiet, a few women screamed and even more men laughed . . . and then came the sound of a man's agonizing cry that rose steadily into the howl of a wolf.

Tommy grabbed Paula's hand hard enough to crush bone. "Jesus," he kept saying. "Jesus. Jesus."

The lights flashed back on and now everyone, including Paula, screamed for all they were worth. In the cage, clothed only in the tattered remains of a pair of jeans, was a huge wolf-like beast, clawing the bars and snarling.

"Ladies and gentlemen, please . . . " the barker yelled. "Be quiet!"

It didn't do any good—especially when the werewolf bent back the bars and leaped out of the cage, landing right in front of Paula.

The audience went wild. Literary. They stampeded, en masse, out of the canvas flap. Tommy, on the other hand, remained exceedingly quiet—he passed out, tumbling onto the sawdust-covered floor like a huge, beached whale.

"Cool," Paula whispered and only eeked once when the were-wolf scooped her up into his hairy, muscular arms and ran out through a back door into the waiting night.

She didn't know where they were going, or how far into the woods they were when he finally stooped and laid her on the soft, leaf-strewn ground. She hadn't been able to take her eyes off the strong muffle and golden, baleful gaze.

"We . . . should . . . be . . . safe . . . here." The werewolf spoke slowly, his jaws barely moving. His voice was a combination of a thick Southern accent and a growl.

"I didn't know werewolves could talk," Paula said.

"It . . . is . . . hard . . . to . . . do . . . when . . . wolf."

"I guess, but could I ask you some questions?"

The shaggy head nodded. Slowly.

"You really are a werewolf?"

Another slow nod.

"God, this is so cool. How long have you been a werewolf? Were you born one or did you get bitten? Do you only change when there's a full moon or whenever you want to? And how come you're with a two-bit carnival instead of running free?"

"Don't . . . have . . . time . . . to . . . talk. Your . . . boyfriend . . . probably . . . already . . . called . . . the . . . cops. Must . . . hurry . . . if we're . . . gonna do . . . it."

"He's not my boyfriend. And what do you mean, if we're going to do it? Who said we're going to do anything?"

The werewolf snorted and gently tore her tank-top apart with one claw. Her little breasts jiggled as he did the same thing to her shorts.

"Hey!"

"Shh," the monster hissed. "Don't . . . you . . . want . . . to?"

Paula thought about it. He had to be better than Tommy, monster or not. "Okay, but you have to answer one question first."

He nodded, his golden eyes focused on the tiny patch of hair between her legs.

"Have you ever met another werewolf?"

He shook his head.

"Oh." Sighing, Paula rolled over and got on all fours, spreading her legs. "What are you waiting for? You do want to do it doggie-style, don't you?"

The werewolf didn't answer. Furry hands on her rump, he entered her with a quick thrust. A dozen strokes later, he let out a less-than-blood-curling howl.

Paula slumped to the ground as he pulled out. It wasn't the best sex she'd ever had, but it wasn't the worse either . . . and it was a whole lot better than anything Tommy could possibly come up with.

Brushing off her hands and knees, Paula walked over to a log and sat down, enjoying the feel of the rough bark against her bare skin. The moon was still low on the horizon and bright orange . . . a Hunter's Moon, they called it.

The werewolf was pissing against a tree . . . only half the monster he'd been a moment before. Still shaggy and lupine from the waist up, his lower half was disappointingly human. And shiny.

"Man . . . that . . . was . . . great," he said as he turned.

That part was disappointingly human, too.

The rubber face-mask made a slurping sound when he peeled it off. It reminded Paula of sneakers against a polished gym floor.

"You're not really a werewolf, are you?"

The young man looked at her as if she'd lost her mind. "Hell, honey, a 'course not. There ain't no such thing."

Paula looked down, dragging her nails against the log.

"Ah, little honey, don't. It's only a trick, like the 'Woman Into Gorilla' . . . I used t'be a magician's assistant, so I can pull the quick change real fast. Todd, the barker, he's my partner, he's the one who came up with the werewolf angle . . . he likes them monster movies, he sure does. You ain't mad, are you?"

Paula shook her head. "No, but it's not nice to make fun of people."

"Oh, little honey," Warren Trudy said, "everybody knows it's fake. We didn't make fun o 'no one."

Paula finally looked up, letting her muzzle extend. It was hard to talk as a wolf, but not that hard.

"Oh . . . yesss . . . you . . . did."

Paula lapped the blood off her pelt and sighed. She really hated to admit it, but Mama was right after all—lean meat was okay once and a while, but you really did have to sink your teeth into something more substantial once and a while.

Scraping the remains of Warren Trudy off her back paws, Paula trotted off toward the carnival parking lot. No doubt that's where Tommy would be . . . waiting for her.

She wouldn't disappoint him this time.

Mike: *The genesis of this story comes from several newspaper stories during the '80s about a Galesburg, Illinois man who died and his family kept him mummified at home for about a decade. They would move him from room to room. Although he was dead he was still part of the family. That real life story of how love survives death kept in the back of my mind for a long time. I also been aching to write my satire of the nuclear family and I knew that Jeffrey Thomas would be the perfect writer to help me write this creepy and funny tale.*

Jeffrey: *It was quite fun working on "Buried With Children." I very seldom collaborate with another author, or write anything of such a blatantly humorous nature, so it was a departure. Another bit of fun for me was writing a zombie story, as I have a great fondness for movies about the living dead in all their permutations. Mike already had the entire story sketched in when it was passed along to me, so it remained for me to flesh it out with my own brand of decomposing flesh. I hope the readers will find this EC Comics-style tale to their own taste!*

BURIED WITH CHILDREN

Michael McCarty and Jeffrey Thomas

Bentley Tench had sat on the bench at the shopping mall all day. That was how he was trying to cope with his soul shattering grief—by watching families have fun, shop and dine at the food court. It had been three weeks since his wife had been killed in the automobile accident.

That in itself could cripple any man's emotions, but she had also been a week from giving birth to triplets. That was what was tormenting him the most—his whole family destroyed by the careless actions of an alcoholic driver. The love of his life and his three children gone, gone, gone.

It just wasn't *fair*. He was a man of science . . . so determined to discover something beneficial to humanity. And then to have this tragedy befall *him* . . .

Bentley had given up science to marry Charlotte. He'd left his low paying position at the college to work at the local nuclear power plant for higher pay. Being a good provider also provided happiness at home. With his increased income, he was able to buy a large house, in the basement of which he had constructed a lab. He still liked to experiment, as he had at the university. He bought state-of-the-art equipment. Cutting-edge computers. That new car . . .

The car that Charlotte's body had been pulled out of.

It was past three o'clock in the morning and he slouched on the sofa, his cigarette having burned down to the filter, but he didn't flick the ashes away . . . leaving the cigarette a long, ashy death stick, like the accusing pointing finger of a child turned to dust.

He tried to lose himself in TV, but there were too many damn commercials, infomercials and lame movies to justify watching this late at night.

Bentley flipped the channel again. 'Night of the Living Dead' was on. He watched the black and white images of a zombie girl killing her mother with a garden trowel, then eating her bloody flesh.

"Well, at least *he* had kids," Bentley said to himself.

More zombies shambled across the TV, almost as stiff as the hosts in those infomercials. Then the little girl killed her father and devoured him, too.

"Yeah, like high amounts of radiation could reanimate the dead," he said to the set. He'd had enough. He turned off the television and went to bed.

Tossing and turning, his sheets soaked with sweat, he still couldn't sleep. Most nights he was lucky if got more then a couple hours of sawing logs.

Abruptly, as if an electric shock had flashed through him, reinvigorating dead nerves, Bentley sat up in his bed. He knew what he had to do. Hadn't he'd known the moment he put his wife in that coffin, that somehow he'd have to try *something* to bring her back to him?

The headlights of his car blazed through the night, his eyes so intense one might think they were the source of the beams.

Bentley broke into the mausoleum on the cemetery grounds . . . gingerly stalked its dark echoing corridors lined with plaques, behind each of which was filed away an eternal slumber. At last, by the ghostly illumination of his flashlight, he found the one plaque marked CHARLOTTE TENCH. With a crowbar he broke into the crypt, with great exertion managed to work out and lower to the marble floor the grimly austere box containing the corpse of his dead wife. Again, he made use of the crowbar to pry off its lid. He felt relief to have had his efforts rewarded . . . even as the tears welled in his eyes to see the condition she was in.

Despite the alchemy of embalming, she was already badly decomposing, perhaps due in part to the summer's oppressive heat wave—her skin greenish-brown in color. Her face was beginning to collapse into itself and wrinkling, and the effluvium released from the box made him choke back a retch.

Nevertheless, he picked up the dead love of his life and the mother of his unborn children and slung her over his shoulder. Gently, as if afraid to wake her prematurely from her slumber, he rested her in the back of the mini van, and he drove her back home. As if she were his new bride again, he carried her over the threshold . . . and then down into the cellar, where he put her body on the table in his lab.

He soon transferred Charlotte to the freezer, in order to stall the process of decomposition.

In the next few days, in a flurry of activity, he stole materials and equipment from work . . . and then installed the spa that he'd bought for his wife and was going to give her on the their fifth wedding anniversary, which was three months away at the time of her early departure from the living.

Having arduously assembled a small-scale nuclear reactor to power the spa, lining the interior of the spa with sheets of lead, and having then filled this tank with nuclear waste smuggled out at great risk, he dubbed his contraction "the foundation of life."

He was ready to take the final step and emerge his dead wife in his own personal recipe for primordial ooze.

Bentley wasn't a religious man. Somehow all the years of science had eroded his belief in God, the Devil, or any superior entity. But he knelt down on the floor of his lab and he prayed. And he cried. Then he prayed some more.

Tenderly he placed Charlotte's naked body into the spa. The room was glowing crimson from the mini-reactor's light, but she still looked lovely in the red radiance and the absinthe-green sludge.

The corpse was bobbing from the power spray jettisoning toxic waste on her.

But nothing was happening. Nothing followed nothing.

It was a failure.

Charlotte let out a bloodcurdling scream and sank to the bottom of the spa.

Bentley ran over to its edge. He was wearing a radiation suit, as there was enough power and waste in his lab to blow up the entire state of Rhode Island.

He dipped his gloved hands in the luminous slime and started fishing for her body.

Charlotte surfaced with a splash, slippery with the green goo dripping off of her. She was holding three crying undead babies in her bloody arms.

"I think this is a nuclear family with one too many split atoms," Bentley said numbly to the zombie babies, as he fed them the raw meat. He had named the trilogy of terror—this unholy trinity—Ethan, Adam and Tom.

Unlike cuddly pink human babies that crave their mother's bosom, the bluish-tinged infant ghouls wanted raw meat. The bloodier the better.

Charlotte divided her time between singing demented nursery rhymes and eating the raw meat as well.

"Jack be nimble
Jack be quick
Jack be tasty
If served with dip.

"Old Mother Hubbard
Went to her cupboard
To fetch her poor dog a bone.
When she got there
The cupboard was bare
And the dog attacked the crone.

"Jack Spratt ate no fat
His zombie wife no lean—
When served human flesh
They licked the platter clean."

Bentley had spent a fortune on steaks, lamb chops, hamburger, veal, bacon, sausage, mutton, pastrami, pork loins and cutlets. He had stocked both the upstairs and downstairs refrigerator and freezer full of meat. But his dead family was famished. Soon their supply was running low.

And if that weren't enough of a concern . . . the undead babies were *growing*. It was normal for infants to grow. But these zombie kids were increasing in mass at a phenomenal rate. They had grown over twenty-four inches in less than a week.

"It must be the radiation," Bentley mused, watching the children play on the floor as he prepared tonight's meal of meatloaf.

Ethan was already taking awkward steps—if with a dragging limp. He looked like his mother more than his father, in that blood was constantly seeping from one or more or all of the holes in his head, and from some that shouldn't even be there. Adam had cute dimples . . . from which streams of yellowish pus continually leaked down his chubby cherubic cheeks. He dragged an umbilical cord that just wouldn't drop off, which he liked to play with and suck on. Tom, by contrast, had a sunken skeletal face . . . and although all three of them were already sprouting teeth, this fact was most evident with Tom because he had no lips to hide them, besides having no eyelids and only a thin membrane for a skin over his clearly defined muscles and veins.

With an exhausted sigh, Bentley turned from his observation of his brood to serve the uncooked meatloaf. The wifey and kids wouldn't eat it unless it was still bloody.

They ripped into the pan, blood and tomato sauce splattering all over the walls.

He had had enough.

"Char, Ethan, Adam, Tom—eat that outside while I clean up this mess," Bentley said sternly. He had figured with it being night, and the back yard being enclosed by a high fence, no one would spot his undead family's eating habits.

He was wrong.

Nosy Mrs. Crabshaw from next door, whilst reading a romance novel by the cool breeze from her living room window, had heard a commotion. She couldn't see what was going on, so she went up to her attic and peered out the narrow windows up there. In her neighbor's back yard, she saw two babies fighting over an old steak bone. That very night, she called human services and reported abuse.

The following morning, a social worker knocked on the Tenchs' door. Bentley answered wearing a robe embroidered over the breast with the motto "#1 Dad" and splattered with blood. He was serving breakfast in the basement. With the stocks of meat running precariously low, the kids were fighting over the last lamb chop.

"Yes?" Bentley said wearily at the door.

"My name is Ted Munson and I work for the state. There's been a reported case of child endangerment; do you mind if I come in—"

"This is a bad time—"

The growls in the basement were getting louder.

"Do you have some kind of dog in the basement?" Ted asked.

"Huh, no—"

Ted brushed past Bentley and went down the stairs. There was half-congealed gore all over the floors and some of the stairs and the social worker slipped down the last five steps . . . snapping his neck in the fall.

Ethan, Adam and Tom pounced on the social worker, tearing at his flesh like sharks in a feeding frenzy. Though his neck was broken, the social worker was still alive for a bit longer. Bentley couldn't see his face, especially since Tom was bent over it, apparently having gotten a hold of a nose or cheek, but Bentley saw the man's legs kick for several moments. Stringy gobs of flesh flew over the triplets' shoulders to strike the floor with wet splats.

Charlotte couldn't contain herself either and joined her kids for breakfast. Growling like a greedy dog competing with her own pups, Bentley's wife dragged one of the man's legs across the floor, leaving a broad swath of scarlet in its wake.

The sight of seeing the social worker devoured by his family was making Bentley nauseous. He went upstairs and poured himself a generous glass of whiskey from the bottle he kept hidden under the counter. He shut the cellar door, because the slurping of the slick intestines, freed from the yawning body cavity, was going to make Bentley lose his own breakfast.

He heard another man's voice screaming.

Bentley went running back downstairs, careful not to slip on the gore as Ted had, however. Apparently there had been another social worker in the car when his partner went inside to investigate . . . and he had entered the basement through the bulkhead door in the yard, drawn by the savage commotion.

This other social worker was hitting Ethan in the head with his briefcase. But Adam and Tom had leaped onto him like leeches and were biting the man.

Ethan clamped onto his hand and he dropped the briefcase.

The man grabbed a pool stick off the table in the recreation room. He swung the cue stick around like some crazed ninja surrounded by samurais with blood-dripping blades.

Charlotte snuck up behind this second man with another cue stick and broke both his neck and Bentley's best stick. The kids and Bentley wife then converged on the poor man like he was some kind of all-you-can eat buffet. Luckily for him, he died about half way through the process.

A school of piranhas could have learned a lot from these ravenous teachers. Within ten minutes, bare bones and tatters of cloth were all that remained of the man . . . and with terrible crunching sounds, they began to work on the bones.

Bentley took the few remaining scraps of clothes of the social workers and threw them in the nuclear hot tub. He also found the keys to Ted's car.

He drove the car ten miles outside the city and walked back home. It was nighttime when Bentley finally arrived.

He was hot and sweaty and even after these hours his stomach was still doing somersaults from what he had witnessed earlier that morning.

He stripped out of his clothes. Lying on the bed already was Charlotte, and she was wearing a sexy nightie. The lacy blue material was see-through, but her decomposing flesh with festering sores was by no means alluring. When she gave him a seductive smile, he saw blackening morsels of flesh wedged between her yellow teeth.

"We've got to do something about those kids; they went too far this time," he said.

"They're kids, dear. Growing kids with a healthy appetite." Charlotte's husky come-hither voice had more to do with the decay of her vocal cords than with amorous effect.

He didn't want to talk about it any further. He pulled up the covers and curled in a fetal position.

He cringed when he felt Charlotte's hand rubbing up and down his back. A bone protruding through her palm scratched him suggestively. "Dear?" she purred.

"Oh, honey . . . I'm sorry . . . I'm tired from my walk," he managed. Though he wasn't sure it was even possible, Bentley suddenly dreaded fertilizing her radiation-steeped undead eggs, making Charlotte pregnant again . . . bringing maybe quadruplets or even quintuplets into the world next time . . .

Bentley woke up around three in the morning. He was plagued

with more nightmares. Ever since he had brought his family back from the dead, it had gotten worse. Sometimes, he lay there thinking, the dead belong . . . well, dead.

He shuffled into the bathroom. Opened the medicine cabinet and popped a couple of aspirins.

They didn't help. His head was pounding like wild conga drums.

He plodded heavily downstairs.

In the bottom of his desk he had kept a Colt .45 semiautomatic for emergencies. And this was one of them.

Too tired for a weepy note to Charlotte, too tired even to feel fear, Bentley Tench lifted the gun to his head and pulled the trigger.

Luckily the blast hadn't woken the babies. Charlotte walked downstairs slowly, partly because she still hadn't worked out all the embalmed stiffness from her muscles, partly because she was afraid of what she saw awaiting her below.

It was gruesome. The gunshot had blown half of her beloved husband's face away.

But ever the resourceful wife, who had never let anything go to waste, Charlotte immediately had an idea of what to do (as soon as she fought back the urge to dig her fingers into that crater in Bentley's face and scoop up some of that beautiful glistening meat). She picked up Bentley's limp and gore-soaked body and dropped it into the fountain of life.

Bentley had no idea why he had tried to kill himself. He was perfectly content with being undead. Of course, being a zombie father helped a lot in raising zombie kids and having a zombie spouse. Now they were all of the same culture and mindset.

The Tenchs sold their house and a heavily made-up Charlotte (it was harder for Bentley to explain away his half a face) purchased them a RV, which they drove around the countryside. At night, they would pull the vehicle to a stop, get out and steal up on some cow sleeping on its feet. Happened so fast the cow didn't even have a chance to moo. They wouldn't leave a drop of blood or any tasty morsels left, not wanting to prompt tales of cattle muti-lations and UFOs; they consumed the entire animal, bones and all. Cow bones were delicious.

"What about pork tomorrow night?" Bentley asked his undead clan after their latest feast.

"Yeah," they cried unanimously. Little Tom even clapped his skeletal hands.

Bentley smiled proudly at his family, and ruffled the gore-sticky hair on Ethan's leaky head. "Good. There are plenty of pig farms in Iowa."

The RV drove over the hill with the moon slowly rising over the horizon, like the shiny dome of some gigantic grinning skull.

Mike: *Charlee Jacob and I are very different writers. However, we did find common ground on the dark tale of suburbia with "The Ice Cream Man." I was heavily influenced by David Cronenberg's creepy classic, The Brood.*

I wrote the first draft of this story in 1990, sent it to the magazine Midnight Zoo—which rejected it—then stuck it in a drawer. It kept gathering dust for almost a decade until I asked Charlee if she could expand the story. It is one of the scariest stories I wrote to date because of the Queen of Hardcore Horror's contribution.

Charlee: *Michael McCarty and I tend to be at opposite ends of the horror spectrum, our points of view being radically different. However, sometimes opposites attract and have something unique to offer one another. When Mike approached me about this project I was curious—for one, because in it I saw a side of Mike I hadn't really seen before. The story contained a germ of genuine nastiness similar to the sorts of things I saw growing up—the sorts of things a child may perceive which may turn him or her with one eye always peering out from the darkness.*

THE ICE CREAM MAN

Michael McCarty & Charlee Jacob

Bad little girls didn't deserve ice cream. Allison Kane was such a girl. She knew it because she was told often enough.

Her mother would say when sufficiently provoked, "Sugar and spice and everything nice isn't you. You're bloodsucking mice and heart full of ice!"

She wore it like a badge of honor. Some kids got stars by their name on the third grade bulletin board—she preferred the skull and crossed bones stickers. When she had to sit in the corner away from the others, she'd blow endless farts just to show her contempt.

At the present moment she was strangling the neighbor's dog, a Milk Dud-eyed spaniel belonging to the funny-smelling old lady next door. It wasn't that she had anything against the dog but she'd seen somewhere on the television that old folks could die suddenly if given a good shock. It was sad the woman had frightened her tenants to death—she'd had three old men die on her in less than a year. She wanted to know how hard it would be to traumatize Mrs. Olson into a heart attack. Then she could get the reputation of being Killer Kane! How cool would that be? She even had a camera set up on the porch, ready to snap an instant picture when the wobbly crone came outside and clutched her chest and went blue.

The pup had stopped whimpering and was just wheezing, chocolate pupils going red, when she let it go because she heard the ice cream van as it turned onto their block. The truck went slow, speakers playing a tinny but cheerful calliope melody as it crept down the suburban street.

Allison dropped the dog and spun, skidding on the shiny green grass. Her tennis shoes pumped. She waved down the truck, her blond pony-tail bouncing as she ran. The ice cream man pulled the vehicle curbside, smiled at her and asked, "Have you been a good little girl?"

Back on the porch, the camera clicked. In a few seconds a photo shot out, showing the back of the white van opening and a gust of cold drifting out on a milky sweet cloud.

Up the street, two boys sat melting plastic soldiers over an anthill. The ants were freaking out, scurrying to and from the opening, trying to build dirt fortifications, dodging blobs of melting green toxins. Nearby sat several empty matchbooks, stacked neatly like creates for munitions.

"I'm sick of this game," Mickey Leland announced to his younger friend. "It's a lame excuse for a war. These plastic soldiers melt too easy. It's too liquidy when it hits 'em. Ought to be heavier than so it's like bombs. Hey, look at that, will ya? When it drips on the anthill it looks like lava. Well, green lava anyway. Not nearly as cool as red 'cause that's the color of blood and fire."

Mickey held the match under the soldier and started with fascination as it dripped and struck the ant fortification, then runneled through it, down the sides of the anthill like down the sides of erupting Mount Popo in Mexico. Ants ran like natives fleeing death.

He smiled. "Like bein' God."

The flame burned back on the match swiftly.

"Ow! I burned my hand . . . " Mickey dropped the match and then stomped on the anthill in fury. No more volcano, no more natives either. God was pissed.

His next-door neighbor, Perry Bradley, scooched back the dirt flew up, squinting his eyes. He watched the older boy stoop and pick up the remaining books of matches.

"I'm gonna go home and play with these by myself," Mickey announced.

"Can I come too, Mickey?" Perry asked meekly. "I like burnin' stuff."

Mickey jerked his head, bringing back a stray lock of red hair that had fallen across his eyes. He sneered. "Naw, get lost. Go play with your sister. You ain't quite up to god-speed, know what I mean? Practice killin' dolls."

Perry whined, jumped up and stood in Mickey's way. "But remember when I shared all my firecrackers with you yesterday?"

"Yeah, so? They're all gone now, lame-o. They were cheap junk anyhow. Half of 'em didn't even go off. Figures—you got 'em from your faggy stepdad."

"He ain't no fag!" Perry cried as Mickey stepped around him and began to walk away.

Mickey swung back around. "Oh yeah? When he ate at our barbecue he crossed his legs like a girl."

Perry glared, little hands bunched into fists. "Did not!"

"Did too," Mickey yelled triumphantly, delighted to see how red in the face Perry was getting. "Yeah, and then our dog scared him. He sissied in the air six feet straight up. Everybody laughed."

Perry bit his lip and blurted, "My dad wouldn't be a'scared of

Jiffy. That mangy overgrown rat a'yours."

Mickey grabbed his crotch and danced around. "No? He just about peed and pooped in his pants when Jiffy barked at him. But he didn't because then other fags wouldn't come around, since they're always out sniffin' each other's butts. Does he sniff your butt? My dad says he does. Says if the welfare only knew."

Perry went pale and nervously rubbed his runny nose. "N-no he don't."

Perry's mom yelled at him from over the fence. "Perry, you come in now and take your bath. Perry? Right now!"

"Okay, Mom," Perry answered reluctantly, not taking his eyes off Mickey.

"Go take a bath, lame-o stepfag. You stink!" Mickey pinched his nose between his fingers and made snorting pig noises. "Or I'll sic Jiffy on ya!"

Perry bent to pick up his soldiers to go home. Mickey jumped ahead of him. "Know what? I'm gonna play with the soldiers too. I'll be the Giant Cyclops Man against the whole U.S. Army. I'll wipe 'em out."

Perry stood with his hands on his skinny hips. He retorted, "Well, if you're gonna play wit *my* soldiers, I get to use your BB gun."

"My butt you do. I ain't got it yet, anyway. I gotta steal some more money from my mom. She gives me money for the church collection but I always keep it see? Just like every week I take quarters out of the basket as it comes 'round the pews. Hey, know why they call 'em pews? Cause they always got butts sittin' on 'em!" Mickey laughed, stuffing Perry's toy soldiers into his pant's pockets.

"That money is for the poor kids," Perry protested, watching as the plastic army men disappeared into Mickey's jeans. Some of them were already partially melted, especially around the heads, like they had been in an atom bomb blast. "I'm gonna tell. You take my soldiers and don't let me play and don't let me use that BB gun and I'm gonna tell Father Pat you take that money."

Mickey leaned close to him and hissed. "Yeah? Well, they don't give it to poor kids. My dad says they finance some terrorist group that blows up poor kids. And if you do tell Father Pat—or anyone—I'll beat your face in. I'll do a God number on you, and you'll be like one of them crushed and burned ants down there on the ground. Take a good look at it and memorize it."

From across the fence came Perry's mom again, yelling in her tired, unhappy voice. "Perry! Perry! Come take your bath!"

"Perry! Perry!" Mickey cried, mocking her. "Your rubber duck's lonely!"

"Knock it off!" Perry warned him, bunched fists coming up.

"Why don't you make me? That is, if you're not a stepfag so's you got somethin' to fight with."

Goaded enough, Perry launched into him. Mickey caught him by the shoulder and pushed him down into the dirt, then jumped on top of him. The two boys started to scuffle without Perry ever able to get the upper hand. Mickey punched him a few times, then rubbed his face into the ruined anthill. When he began blowing bloody snot the bigger boy let him up.

"Go take your bath, sissy-lips," Mickey barked. "Be sure to try on that new frilly dress your fagdad made for ya so you two can get married."

"Mom!" Perry cried, running off sobbing dusty tears and spitting out gobs of green plastic melt-goop. "Mickey pushed me down real hard."

"Wah, wah, wah," Mickey shouted. "Go cry to your mommy. Tell her I pushed your face into the ant's graveyard. And when I get my BB gun, I'm gonna shoot your cat! Make you eat its brains! Make a real man outta ya!"

The glass patio door slid open and Mickey's dad appeared, silhouetted in the entranceway. The shadow called out sternly, "Mickey, come inside this very minute."

Mickey bowed his head and felt some invisible tail tuck between his legs like he'd seen Jiffy's do when the dog had been caught peeing on the carpet.

"Coming, Dad," he replied as obediently as he could muster. He slinked into the house, rolling his eyes when he was sure his father couldn't see him.

"Sit down over there, boy," his father directed, pointing to the sofa. "Now I saw what you did just now to Perry and—"

Mickey huffed. "Aw, dad . . . "

"Don't give me any of your lip. I'm not little like Perry and I won't be pushed down into the dirt. You listen to me, son," his father began, voice rising in anger. "There's no excuse for what you did to that boy. Right now I feel like using the buckle end of my belt over you. You rightly deserve a few licks. Spare the rod and spoil the child maybe, but I just believe that it wouldn't do any good. It hasn't before."

The old man paused, deliberating. Mickey could detect the righteous wheels going round inside his father's head. "I'm gong to tell you a story instead."

"Aw, please, not more of that Bible crap," Mickey spat back. "Just beat me. It's better than bein' bored any day."

Mr. Leland slapped his son across the face. The sting snapped his head to a sharp right and made the boy start crying quietly, trying to hold it in but unable to.

His father waited until he heard a few satisfying hitches that guaranteed he had the kid's attention then he continued with his lecture. "Don't make fun of The Bible, Son. Your mother and I live our lives based on the Good Book. You respect that as you respect us. Hey, you think this is funny?"

Mickey realized he'd smirked and knew that was a mistake as another slap straightened him in his chair.

"God isn't a comedian, I assure you," his father said. "Now once there were two boys who lived in a neighborhood like this one. Same kind of families, same chance to do the right thing, but one turned out good, the other bad. Do you hear me?"

"Yes . . . " Mickey said, still furious at being overcome by sobs. He'd rather have spit in the old man's eyes. He clenched his muscles, not unlike straining to hold it in when he had to go to the bathroom but was forced to sit still in school or church instead. Not wanting to shiver or tremble. Not wanting his dad to have power over him. He put up a wall so he couldn't really hear anything his father was saying, just giving an affirmation now and then to make the old guy think he was listening when really he was imagining himself to be God (or a demon would do just as nicely), raining down hot lava on helpless villagers living below Mount PoPo. PoPo! What a funny name. A baby's word for butt was what that was.

" . . . and that bad boy was taken away on the back of the black dog which howled until the gate of hell opened up to let them in," his father said, staring at him.

Mickey realized the story was over. Usual grisly parable about Good Deeds and Retribution and how God was not a very funny guy. Not that this story was quite out of The Bible, but the old man knew the times called for updated material.

"I'm extremely disappointed in you, Mickey," his father finished up. "You only care about yourself. I want to think about what you did. I don't want anything like this to happen again. You're grounded, so stay in your room for the rest of the day. Tomorrow you will apologize to Perry and use the money you've saved up for your gun to buy him new soldiers."

Mickey's jaw dropped. "Dad! You've gotta be joking . . . "

His father cocked his head. "I don't hear God laughing. Do you?"

Mickey shared a large bedroom with his younger brother Matt. The room was decked out with posters of Britney Spears, Bart Simpson, The X-Men, The Incredible Hulk, Spider-Man and Harry Potter.

In the center of the room was an entertainment center with 20" screen TV, DVD player and X-Box player. Game cassettes were scattered all over the room.

Mickey sat sulking on his bed. Jiffy padded up and then jumped onto the bed. The terrier inched close to the young redhead and licked his hand, trying to cheer him up.

"Go away, Jiffy," Mickey ordered, jerking his hand and away and wiping the wet fingers on the spread.

The dog ignored his request and stretched out on the bed

beside him, tail thumping against the mattress.

Mickey kicked him. Jiffy let out a long howl and sought refuge under Matt's bed. The bedroom door was closed so he couldn't just run out. Mickey leaped down, hunkering on the floor, peering under his brother's bed, seeking to further torment the pet. The dog growled at him.

Mickey then spotted Matt's Scooby-Doo bank half-buried underneath a stack of Spawn comic books, stuffed under the bed to keep Mickey out of them, no doubt. He wiggled under, grabbing hold of the bank. Then he dragged it out and smashed it open, stuffing the dollar bills and coins into his pockets—after first getting rid of the plastic soldiers.

"Hot damn! This should be enough to get my BB gun. Then watch out, cat!"

He quietly opened the bedroom window and slipped outside unnoticed. Seeing the coast was clear, he ran across the backyard, through the neighbor's lawn, stopping at the end of the block at a vacant lot.

He ran for another couple of blocks, taking a breather in front of old man Rutherford's house. Joe Rutherford, a retired roofer, lived next to the Sunnyside Assembly Of God church and he had a bad reputation among the neighborhood kids.

It was known that Joe's cheating wife had run out on him but it was rumored he'd cut her up and buried her all around the yard. Mickey and some of the other children got together one night and went looking for the pieces. He caught them after there were about fifteen deep holes all over, with many of the trees and flowers ruined. He called the cops and made a ruckus, threatening to sue all their parents.

"Now, now," Sergeant Alan Pierce had said, trying to calm the big man down. "They're just kids. Laugh it off."

"People round about here don't chuckle a lot, Officer," Joe had answered. "Don't really have a lot to find funny."

They got whippings. And Joe just put up a lot of homemade stew in glass jars. Was always cooking up more and it made the whole block stink of blood sometimes. Sold it to a restaurant downtown and brought it to all the block barbecues.

Now Mickey realized where he was, smelling that weird sweet-salt meat stench, kind of pork, kind of like really cheap perfume. He started to run away when a wicked idea jolted him. He could see a stack of the newly filled Mason jars cooling on a table through an open kitchen window. There were rocks piled up around recently planted saplings in the front yard. Mickey used them to throw at the jars, pitching one after another until he hit the mark and the stack collapsed off the table and onto the floor.

Amid the sounds of shattering glass, Rutherford bellowed from inside the house, "What the hell is going on out–"

Before Rutherford could finish his sentence, Mickey was long gone. When he was sure he was safe, he stopped again.

A familiar sound caught his ears. He heard calliope music, oompah-pah, oompah-pah. He spotted the ice cream truck slowly driving down the street, solemn as a funeral procession except for the happy music. He had the sudden urge for a snow cone.

He waved with his arms. "Hey! Over here!"

The ice cream truck came to a halt by the curb, and Mickey walked toward the vehicle to scan the selections and prices posted. The driver got out and walked around to the back.

"I scream, you scream, we all scream for ice cream," he said as the boy approached him. The lanky man wore immaculate white clothes. He was completely bald, scalp like shiny wax. His was a common face except for big lips and a perfectly straight nose. His dull gray eyes were set deep in his head. Not a clown's face, that was for sure.

The ice cream man smiled. "It's mighty hot out today. Perfect weather for ice cream, don't you think?"

"Yeah," Mickey agreed. "Hot enough to melt an M&M in your hand before it reaches your mouth."

The ice cream man began to laugh. And laugh and laugh.

"Damn, it ain't that funny," Mickey muttered under his breath.

Blood started to trickle from the driver's ears.

Mickey stared, startled, sure it was a trick. The ice cream man roared with laughter as his face melted. His skin oozed from his head as off a giant scoop of vanilla, dripping down onto the pavement. His deteriorating flesh liquified like the biggest cone ever, nose dissolving into a milk-slimy puddle. The vendor kept laughing even after his lips fell off his face to splash on Mickey's new Nikes.

The face was now nothing more than a skull covered with grease and blood. "You crack me up, kid." How he said it was a mystery. The teeth clacked like frozen, pearly gummy bears.

Mickey looked down at his shoes. The lips appeared to be made of some kind of hard sugar, like sprinkles but glossier, staining the Nikes with too much food coloring. The kid was breathless with shock. He turned to get the hell away but it was too late. The ice cream man grabbed the youth with one hand and lifted him high into the air.

"Let me down," Mickey screamed.

The vendor opened the back of the truck with his free hand. Cold vapors escaped and vanished into the scorching heat as the ice cream man tossed the boy into the back of the van. The locks were quickly bolted.

It was very dark and cold in the back of the truck. Panic struck as Mickey hammered his fists against the steel doors. "Let me out of here, you freak!"

Searching his pockets, he found one of the matchbooks he had used to melt the soldiers with. He lit a match and looked around. He couldn't believe what he saw.

The back of the ice cream truck looked like a meat locker. But instead of slabs of meat, it was filled with the frozen bodies of little boys and girls.

The back window on the driver's side opened and the bloody skull of the ice cream man appeared. "I'm taking you to where all the bad boys and girls go. The Land of the Frozen Dead."

Mickey tried to beg. "No, please . . . "

The vendor quickly shut the window. He started the truck. The rumble of the engine felt like an Arctic earthquake.

The presence of death blew through the interior of the van in frigid gusts. Mickey felt the coldness numb his skin. The bodies of the boys and girls swayed back and forth as the ice cream truck sped down the road—no stately pace now.

The back window opened again and the slimy skull reappeared. "Chilling out? Don't worry—cold hands, warm heart."

The creature laughed again before slamming the window shut.

Mickey was forced to sit down on his own feet or be thrown down as the van picked up more speed. He wrapped his arms around his legs and tried to make himself warm. Suddenly, a movement caught Mickey's eyes.

A finger on the body of a frozen girl started to twitch. Her hands were shaking, then her arms. She was soon shuddering from head to foot. She grunted and put her hands up to lift herself off the hook from which her body had been suspended. She hit the floor with a dull thump.

She turned to Mickey and stared at him with empty eyes.

No, he thought, they weren't quite empty. They had plenty of murder in them.

The girl coming down started a domino effect. The others started shaking and trembling, lifting themselves off the meat hooks and landing on the floor of the van on hard, gray-blue feet.

The dead boys and girls moved slowly toward Mickey. "I scream, you scream, we all scream for ice cream," they whispered in unison.

He slid toward the back of the truck but was soon cornered. They touched him with their icy fingers. Mickey felt frozen meat wrap around his throat. He started screaming, but it wasn't for ice cream.

The boy's shrieks weren't heard by the commuters, coming home from a hard day's work in the city. Nor were they heard by people cutting or watering their well-manicured lawns. The boy's cries for help weren't within earshot of any of the backyard barbecues.

Life in the suburbs went on as it always did. The ice cream man kept driving down the road, smiling and laughing all the way.

He was, after all, the Good Humor Man.

Mike: *Cristopher Hennessey-DeRose and I collaborated on several interviews — some of them can be found in* Giants Of The Genre. *One day Criss called me on the phone and told me he had this idea of a story about a comic book super-hero/super-villain city and the humans that had to keep it clean. I probably read too many comic books to live a normal life, so I had no problem writing up the story. Criss came up with some early clever twists. I think this story would make a great comic book or graphic novel.*

Criss: *It just seemed like a fun idea that would suit Mike's quirky sense of humor. Once he showed me what he wrote, I was able to basically ride roughshod over it with some observations (some may say 'cynical pissings'). I've been gloomy since the bottom fell out of the comic industry some years ago. I'm just now getting over it.*

SUPER-CLEAN

Cristopher Hennessey-DeRose & Michael McCarty

Super-City was a super mess.

The metropolis of the superheroes and supervillains was super-trashed. Both the crime-fighters and the criminals agreed their megalopolis was in desperate need of cleaning. The daily rumbles had taken its toll: knocked-over billboards, busted windows, all kinds of debris littered the streets and parks.

Who would clean it?

The supervillains were too busy trying to steal shit and take over the world, and the superheroes were too busy trying to stop them, as well as posing for photos for fans and settling trademark disputes with other superheroes. Product endorsement was the sole common ground of villains and heroes alike, and who could blame them? The Black Vise didn't want to be seen drinking the same soda as a do-gooder like Captain Forever, whose codpiece continued to grow with each public appearance, much to the delight and debate of normals and super-beings alike.

The Super-City City Council met, discussed the situation, and reached a unanimous conclusion: hire humans to do the cleaning.

You read that correctly. Humans.

Mortals.

Homo Sapiens.

Controversy on a plate.

Those disgusting creatures who, when cut, would bleed — and when they died, their bodies would stiffen and stink, and, unlike the superbeings, wouldn't rise from the dead — even though there was no possible way for them to have survived a blast point-blank from the evil Dr. Fang's End-All Gun. The leader of the controversial superteam Crimekillers U.K., Mr. Quasi, should never have recovered from his supposed "genuine and tragic" death, the likes of which hadn't been seen since a certain popular singer went teats-up in Tupelo.

Super-City was sturdy: it could survive cars being thrown around like paper airplanes and occasions like the time Scum-Boy had to make an emergency landing in his aircraft — which most called 'The Flying Bag of Crap' — into the city's precious water supply. But the City Council had to think about plummeting property values, so a bail-out that would make Southern California Edison drool was not contested.

But they couldn't let mere mortals go gallivanting all around like unsupervised children in an adult world. Well, they could, actually, but the city's insurance premiums would've increased a bit too much, to say nothing about the labor laws regarding such things.

It was decided they would hire one of their own to take charge of the operation: the Faceless Man, a former superhero who lost his face shaving with a nuclear-powered razor that had been tampered with by the aforementioned Dr. Fang. The choice gave fire to a brief but heated debate about potential abuse of power, as he did have a history of chaos and general strife-making during his brief stint as a supervillain. But because he had no face, they couldn't put his mug on the cover of comic books, so they gave him the new position so he could stop being Unemployed Faceless Man. The debate ended with not so much as a whimper when it became obvious that no one else wanted the job.

Because of budget cutbacks, he could only hire three employees. As it turned out, only four people applied anyway. During the interviews, Faceless soon discovered that Stan the Slacker hadn't really wanted the job. He had only filled out the application to continue his unemployment benefits. His habit of taking naps during interviews and peppering his conversation with words like "Dude" only made his chances of finding a job worse.

So Faceless hired the other three candidates. Moped-Head Mama was a middle-aged woman who rode on a moped to do cleaning. She could attach mops, brooms, vacuum cleaners and portal trash cans to the moped.

Hook was a young man who had lost his right hand in a bet. He had wagered a contortionist that he couldn't lick his own balls. He'd lost and so off went the hand. Exactly why he had wagered his hand—or at least the entire thing, as opposed to just a finger or two—in what many had considered a sucker bet (no pun intended), would become the source of endless speculation.

The Stinker was an old man who lived in the sewers all his life. He didn't mind cleaning, as long as soap and water didn't have to hit his body in order for him to do job. Moped-Head had to sign a notarized agreement saying that she would stay at least twelve feet away from him at all times.

They became The Clean Team, and it was their job to keep Super-City super-clean.

Here is this issue's adventure:

Faceless: Clean Team, read my lips. We have big trouble. Big.

Stinker: But boss, you have no lips—

Hook: As a matter of fact, I'm kinda surprised you can even SEE us, let alone speak . . .

 No offense, boss.

Faceless: None taken. Ahem. The Super-Comic Book Factory

has been super-trashed again.

Moped-Head: Who fought this time?

Faceless: The supervillains were Ratman, Radioactive Man, Rubberneck Woman and the Slimester.

Hook: Not the Slimester! His stains are next to impossible to get out.

Faceless: The Superheroes were Hippie Wolfman, Cactus Woman, The Invisible Viking and The Singing Dwarf. It was quite a rumble.

Stinker: Hippie Wolfman, he's not even housebroken. I'm not sure why they let him fight inside.

Hook: The Singing Dwarf isn't much better. Remember that time Ratman had him against the wall of Super-Hall? The Dwarf only made things worse by singing selections from 'Cats' and 'Starlight Express.'

Faceless: Right, we all remember that, but—

Hook: It only made a bad situation worse, didn't it? I mean, that just pissed off Ratman even more.

Moped-Head: Took me forever to get the stains off that wall.

Faceless: Gang?

Hook: He just beat hell out of the Dwarf. Probably would've let the poor little guy go after a while—

Faceless: We all remember. Now then —

Hook: But he just pounded the little guy right into the ground. Remember? It took all of us plus a couple guys on the street to pull him out.

Faceless: Hook!

Hook: If it hadn't been for MegaDude, the Battlin' Surfer, the Dwarf would've been finished!

Moped-Head: He was pretty beat up. Didn't even know who we were.

Faceless: Exactly when did I lose control of the situation here?

Hook: Broke his wristwatch and everything . . .

Faceless: Quit your complaining, gang! It's time we do some deep cleaning and fast. As I like to say—

Moped-Head, Stinker and Hook (in unison): "There are the

cleaners and the leaners—and they aren't paying us to lean."

Faceless: Actually I was going to say, try to get the job done in eight hours. I hate paying overtime.

The Clean Team took the Clean-Mobile, a bookmobile that had been converted into a cleaning vehicle, equipped with their cleaning supplies, equipment and special gadgets and formulas, including various 'experimental' cleaning agents.

When they pulled into the parking lot, it was covered with comic books.

The cops tried their best to keep drooling comic book collectors and dweebs away from such treasures as issue #1 of Ratman Goes Into The Cellar, or the super-rare Hippie Wolfman Gets His Rabies Shot (issue #891) and the priceless The Singing Dwarf Sings ABBA's Greatest Hits (Issue 69—only two copies are known to be in existence). A photo cover of the first issue of the short-lived series, The Invisible Viking & Kelp-Boy was among those books reduced to mere Near-Mint status. Certain collectors who, as far as anybody had seen, never actually bought anything, would turn their noses up at such pathetic displays of preservation, picking out imperfections with a jeweler's eye before tossing them back into the pile more dismissively than an English judge.

Moped-Head Mama cleaned the parking lot with her moped's special attached broom and dustpan in about thirty minutes—a hell of a lot longer than a speeding bullet. Middle-aged men tried like hell to get the last copy of SoCal, Man Without Sunscreen #41 (The rare one, although none of them could tell you exactly why. It just said so in the beat-up copy of the Bible of Comic Book Price Guides they all carried in their backpacks, so there but for the grace of mylar sleeves went they). But they cried like—well, middle-aged comic book collectors as it was folded, spindled and severely mutilated by Moped-Head's cleaning efforts. There were sounds that could only be referred to as 'plaintive wails' when she whipped out her Patent-Pending Bionic Beater Bar attachment and sucked up all that remained of the four-color pages. Everything from splitting profits to sexual favors were offered to her if she would only "EMPTY OUT THE GODDAMN BAG!" as several of the men were quoted as saying.

The Clean Team entered the factory.

The first thing they saw was a glowing soda can.

"Must have been something the Radioactive Man drank," Stinker commented. "I have some special gloves back in The Clean-Mobile—"

"No need." Hook said. He picked the can up with his hook and tossed it into his garbage bag.

They split up.

Moped-Head Mama cleaned up the cactus needles and cactus juice in the hallways while keeping a sharp eye out for any evil-doers looking for peyote.

Hook cleaned up the slimy trail of the Slimester.

And Stinker had the unfortunate duty of cleaning up the wolf shit and radioactive waste. Sometimes it's not easy being a Stinker... he would later complain that his testicles glowed in the dark, something Moped-Head seemed to find interesting enough to ask for pictures and for some reason, a signed doctor's declaration of some kind.

On the surface, it was an ordinary day for the Team. But it was a historical day, too, for one collector who was bitten by what some say must have been a radioactive gnat as he reached for what was perhaps the finest-looking copy of Morph Man Special #1. In a flash, he was turned into Pristine-Mint Man, able to see small, insignificant perfections in anything a mile off and carry twice the annoyance factor associated with the gnat.

But that's a different story entirely. The factory itself looked like new. Well, almost.

Back at Clean Team Headquarters:

Faceless: Clean Team, you did a super job cleaning the factory. Even cleaned up that hard-to-remove comic book ink. But there was a major confrontation in Superhero Park—statues were spray-painted with graffiti, waste-baskets were set on fire—and litter, oh so much litter. And I don't know how we're going to get that cat down from that tree... Are you up for the job?

Moped-Head, Hook & Stinker (together): Yes!

Next issue:

Will the Clean Team finally meet their match when they battle the Incredible Grime Master? Will they be overcome by The Sludge That Wouldn't Die?

Stay tuned ...

Mike: *I knew Sandra DeLuca for years as the editor of Goddess Of The Bay and Requiem (I wrote the first poem for the premiere issue). I first met Sandy at the World Horror Convention in Denver. About a year later, when I was vacationing at Minneapolis, she e-mailed me this story and asked if I'd like to expanded it. Usually it's the other way around, so I was happy to write a tale from the receiving end instead of the sender's end. Sandy is also a very talented artist, which explains why the protagonist, a struggling art student, is written with such realism.*

Sandy: *I've been fascinated with dark angels for many years and have done extensive research on fallen angels, demonic angels and the Angel of Death, just to name a few. It's interesting to note that biblical angels, angels from The Book of Enoch and post-biblical literature usually portray these beings as male. This holds true for much of the information I've gleaned from transcripts written by early Christians and Jews.*

Of course a woman can do anything just as well as a man. Thus, why can't one of us be the Angel of Death? Mira fits the role perfectly. In addition, she's hip and beautiful.

Mira was born within my imagination a few years ago. She flitted around for a while and came to life on paper. She was cool. She was hot. However, the story lacked something: a spark I just could kindle no matter how hard I tried. This sort of thing happens to writers at times. When it does the word collaboration make a great deal of sense.

Michael McCarty is a master at creating magical dialogue and adding a bit of color to a tale — the kind of dialogue and color that my little Mira was lacking. So one cold February morning I sent him the manuscript. He sent it back a week later. And wouldn't you know it? Mira's story was finally complete.

MIRA

Sandra DeLuca and Michael McCarty

Each evening I sat outside Pandora's Coffee Box, staring into a cup of coffee as black as a starless night. As black as my soul. As black as Death.

Everything else on Thayer Street was alive with bright colors—especially red, white and blue. Everything in 1976 was centered around the Bicentennial, the 200th birthday of the Declaration of Independence. You couldn't escape it. Every day there was some fresh bit of news about the Bicentennial. It seemed like one big surprise party was going to happen in one month—but it was hardly a surprise.

Even my follow art students, who normally wore dark, drab clothes, suddenly began sporting bright pins and painting flags on their wardrobe. I was so sick of it all that I felt like vomiting, but knowing my luck, that too would be red, white and blue.

No, I didn't share the country's celebratory mood. Being an artist, I was always a little off-center. I stared into my black coffee as students discussed paintings on display in the Rhode Island School of Design museum on Benefit Street. Sometimes I gazed across the street into the windows of Pyramid Books, where crystals and chimes dangled.

One student carried a radio down the street that blared The Eagles' "Hotel California." It was definitely an Eagles' summer. They dominated the FM airwaves. Whether it was the title track, "New Kid In Town," or "Life In The Fast Lane," you couldn't escape the Eagles, no more than you could escape the Bicentennial.

As cars passed by, Don Henley's voice could be heard in every direction. He sang about smelly warm colitas. What the hell is a colita anyway?

I only waited for Mira to appear, when the sun sank beneath the horizon.

As if on cue, when bells tolled from Saint Francis Cathedral, below in the heart of the city, she turned the corner. Mira. Her auburn hair swirled in the wind, dark eyes sparkled as she looked to the moon. Her long skirt was slit to the hip, revealing black lace garter, silver flask tucked inside.

She nodded as she passed by. Nobody turned or even seemed to notice her stroll past Avon Cinema, past The College Hill Bookstore and turn the corner onto Angell Street. I rose from my table, following her flowery scent—as I had done for two weeks since the accident.

It had been late Spring. A small red sports car had swerved around the corner, its headlights blazing like demon eyes, brakes screeching. The vehicle hit me as I crossed Thayer, hurtling me onto hard pavement. The driver, a bleached blonde in a skimpy dress and clog sandals, opened the car door, looked at me, screamed. A man raced across the street to a phone booth. Others crowded around me. I tried to look up at all the faces, but there was too much blood in my eyes. All I could really see was the horror in their expressions. I couldn't believe I'd been hit by a car, it had happened so fast. I remember wondering why I wasn't dead.

There I was, sprawled in the middle of the street, head pounding, too shocked to scream. Then I saw her for the first time—an angel, hovering over me, a small silver flask in her hand.

She was so beautiful. I didn't care that I was bleeding to death. It didn't matter when she stood next to me.

"You're so beautiful," I stammered around a mouthful of blood.

"It's not your time, Josh," she whispered. Her dark eyes burned through me.

Time? I was disoriented. Did she want to know what time it was? Or maybe, like a parking meter's bought time, my expiration was still a nickel away. I reached for her, mesmerized by her ethereal face. She shook her head slowly.

It felt so right to be near her, but at the same time it was very wrong to be so in love with this dark angel . . . like getting an erection at a funeral.

Mist enveloped her. A paramedic lifted me gently onto a stretcher.

Two weeks later, they released me from the hospital. I went back to my old haunts on the East Side of Providence. I soon realized that the lovely angel of death had returned as well.

She appeared one night as I read Chekov in a corner booth at Andrea's.

"My angel," I whispered. "My dark angel. I've been waiting for you so long. What's your name?"

"Mira," she said.

"Even your name is beautiful. My soul is on fire, and only you can extinguish the flames."

She looked away. "I have no time for some mortal drooling over me. Go back to the living."

Some noisy students entered the room and I glanced their way. When I turned back to Mira, she was gone.

I couldn't stop thinking about her. She was perfection. I thought about making love to her, dancing through the night with her . . .

Now I followed as she approached an old man—a streetperson, lying in the doorway of a vintage clothing store. He clenched an empty whiskey bottle. Drool ran down his chin.

Mira stopped before him, bent down to stroke his withered cheek. Pulling the flask from her garter, she whispered something in his ear, then raised the flask to his lips.

He drank.

Then his breathing stopped.

A second later, he was just another old panhandler who had passed away during a summer heatwave. Just another paragraph in the obituaries, and a short paragraph at that. Just another statistic in one of countless reports on the homeless problem.

His spirit spiraled upward. He gazed down at her, smiled peacefully, drifted away.

She threw him a seductive kiss. "Meet you on the other side."

I caught up with her. "Mira, take me with you to that other side."

She laughed, deep and throaty, throwing back her head. "You again! Josh Crandall, I've already told you: It's not your time. Get paint on your jeans, in your hair. Live."

"But I love you." I fished a joint out of an inside jacket pocket.

"Let's get high and make love all night."

She laughed and shook her head.

"But I can see you, Mira. None of the others can. That must mean something."

"It just means you're a sensitive guy—special—destined to be a cool painter. It also means you're thinking of me in ways you shouldn't." She tossed her thick, auburn locks. "Your destiny is waiting."

"My destiny is you."

She sighed. "Look, Josh. I have work to do. Why don't we meet later in the park? I'll think about what you said. Okay, kid?"

Kid. That made me feel about eight years old. But only for a moment. "By the carousel?"

"Um, yeah, that's cool. I'll meet you there." She looked to the moon. "Make it around four in the morning. My shift'll be over by then."

The hours passed slowly. I went to a crowded coffee house and listened to poets recite verse about death, darkness, lost love . . . Such amateurs. They wrote about darkness, but all had day-jobs.

I ached for Mira.

At 3:30 I hailed a cab, asked him to drive me to Roger Williams Park.

"A little late for a picnic?" he spat.

"Just take me there. Mira's waiting."

"Hooker or something?"

"Just drive. Here's twenty bucks up front."

"Sure. Like they say, 'Money talks, bullshit walks.' And as a cabbie, I don't like 'em walking."

It was four in the morning. The carousel house blazed with light. Tinkling organ music flowed from open doors. Brightly colored ponies spun round.

I saw Mira perched on a black stallion. She waved as she whirled by. I waved back, in awe of her, knowing she'd created this illusion– this magic—for me.

The music faded, lights dimmed, the carousel ceased turning.

"What do you want from me, Josh?"

"I want to love you, Mira. I want to be with you for all eternity."

"Get a grip, kid. I'm an angel of death—not the kind of girl you take home to mother. Besides, eternity is a long time. I should know."

"Ever since I saw you—the night of the accident—I've wanted you. You are my cold winter in a windswept graveyard. You are my nights with a full moon. You are the void in my dark, aching soul." I touched her cheek. It was cold against my face . . . too cold for June.

She sighed. Her eyes welled with tears. "It's been lonely. I admit it. But it wasn't your time that night—or tonight. It won't be for years."

"I'm lonely too, Mira."

"It's been so empty," she said softly. She took my hands, leading me into a tangle of trees. She kissed me deeply, her tongue darting, teasing, slithering like a snake into the pit of my mouth.

Clothes melted from her body, revealing alabaster skin, large, firm breasts. We fell to the ground, made love gently at first. She moved slowly beneath me, but soon her movements became quicker, harder. Her nails dug into my back.

Afterward, we rested next to each other in silence. Then Mira turned and stared at me. Her eyes held the faces of the dead, those she had taken. I saw loneliness, pain, mourning. She was a ghostly specter tortured by empty years, touched by darkness. "I haven't changed my mind, you know," she said. "I have my work to do. But I thank you—I have been comforting others for so long that I'd forgotten that I have needs, too. But you have your whole future ahead of you. Go on with your life, Josh. Go."

And so I left her. Rain began to beat down on me, slapping my face. I ran until I was back in the city, inside my apartment, bolting the door. I slid to the floor and cried—for Mira. I would never forget that wild, intense night—ever.

I've painted her face, her essence—her world—countless times over the past twenty-four years. She has haunted me all this time, drifted within my dreams as her tongue danced in my mouth, as her hands seduced my body.

So many paintings. They surround me here in my studio. They hang in galleries throughout the world. Her memory inspired them all. She has given me wealth, fame—but the sadness remains. I've tried to drink away the pain. But the pain remains, and my liver is nearly destroyed.

I gaze at the empty street from my window. The sun sinks beneath the horizon.

As if on cue, bells toll from Saint Francis Cathedral, below in the heart of the city. I gasp as she turns the corner—Mira. Her auburn hair swirls in the summer wind, her dark eyes dazzle as she looks to the moon. Her long skirt is slit to the hip, revealing black lace garter, a silver flask tucked inside.

I gather my jacket, cap and cane. I make my way into the street. A red sports car speeds around the corner, headlights blazing, and sends me flying like a broken puppet. My head pounds, pain blazes in my body, but I'm far too happy to scream.

I drink sweetness from the shining flask. Thank you, Mira.

This time, it will be forever.

Mike : *Mark and I wrote this story for Shane Ryan Staley's anthology,*
Dark Testament. Shane wanted a Bible-inspired tale that was very dark,
and I remembered the story of Legion — I thought that was pretty creepy
material. Plus, I'd always loved Frederik Pohl's "social-science fiction"
and wanted to do a dark version of that. This story received an Honorable
Mention in the 2002 edition of The Year's Best Fantasy And Horror. I
think this is one of the darkest tales Mark and I have written together.

Mark: *This is a very serious, grim story, and yet it is oddly optimistic.*
The future is a horrible wasteland, yet people are still hanging on, doing
whatever it takes to survive. That, I think, is an incredible aspect of hu-
man existence. We keep on keepin' on, even when we're fighting against
Nature — or each other. That's rather amazing, when you consider that
each of us is just a mess of bones, muscles and soggy organs, held together
in a soft sack of skin. We don't even have exterior plating, like bugs. And
yet we survive. Pretty good for a bunch of squishy skin-sacks.

CITY OF TWO-THOUSAND SINS

Michael McCarty and Mark McLaughlin

It was a city without a name.

Desert sands had buried the name of the city years ago. But
most cities these days had no names anyway. After the depletion
of all fossil fuel resources in 2060, the collapse of the world
economy and the nuclear war in Mexico, North America was in
ruins. Global warming completed the picture by baking the
once-prosperous land into a barren dustbowl.

And names. Names weren't a high priority anymore. One
shithole settlement was pretty much the same as the next: no food,
no water, no power, nothing.

At one time, the city must have been a place of opulence and
excitement. Traces of its former glory could be seen everywhere.
Marble walls and fountains. Crystal chandeliers. The ruins of

gaming tables, stages and bars—yes, people had once had fun in this city.

But the days of fun and games were long gone.

Jeb was the official sin-counter.

He was a tall, dark-bearded man with rugged features and surprisingly gentle eyes. He had numbers tattooed all over his body. On his face, he had a '24' on one cheek and a '7' on the other, with a '365' on his forehead. He had a '111' on each palm and a '222' on the sole of each foot.

His task was to count the sins of those who dwelled in the nameless city. He recorded them all in his Sin Book, which rested on a podium in the Great Hall. This Hall, the spiritual center of their community, was the enormous lobby of their casino-hotel-church.

Each Sunday, he would read and number the sins.

"Sin one-thousand, nine-hundred and ninety-seven: Noah slept well past noon and did not do his morning chores," Jeb read. He smiled as he handed Noah a red token.

The gathering crowd mumbled their approval.

"Sin one-thousand, nine-hundred and ninety-eight: Jonah ate bread without giving thanks," Jeb read.

"That isn't a sin," Cain complained. "It was not a meal. One does not need to give thanks every time one eats some small morsel."

"I'm too hungry to care," Samuel rasped between dry, cracked lips.

The sunny days roasted the flesh and the windswept nights chilled it to the bone.

At one point, after the power went out, Herod removed all the Bibles from the hotel rooms and burned them in trash cans inside a supermarket. He had appointed himself leader, and he'd thought this action would serve his people well. After all, people were more important than books. The blaze kept everyone there warm all night. The previous night they had used menus and playing cards. Those hadn't burned well because of their heavy lamination. They gave off sickening fumes and many people became ill. But the Bibles had burned splendidly. They kept everyone nice and warm.

Eventually the people turned against Herod. He hadn't done anything wrong ... But still, they needed to vent their frustration with the world somehow, and his helpfulness—his patient optimism in the face of maddening despair—had become an annoyance.

A group assigned to the task tied him down outside of the tallest building in the city. Then they went up to the top and starting dropping things down on him out of a penthouse window. There was no special significance in this particular form of torture: it just seemed like the thing to do at the time. In the end Herod was reduced to a pile of human slush embedded with a medley of broken everyday objects—everything from wine glasses to typewriters.

"You know the rules, Cain," Jeb said. "If we all don't agree that a particular act is a sin, then it has to be put to a vote."

"Please, don't," David begged. "Let's not waste time—I'm famished. The last thing I put in my mouth was a cockroach I'd caught, and I threw up a minute later. I'm so hungry. I'll die if I don't get some food soon."

"I don't make the rules," Jeb said. "I just count the sins. And I shall always do so, until the day we are all too weak to even move. It is my task. I answer to a higher power." So saying, he looked up, as did everyone else in the Great Hall.

There was a time, in the early days after the chaos started, when the people in the town went a little crazy. The death of Herod set the pace for even more bizarre acts of cruelty, prejudice, and—more often than not—perverse righteousness.

Angry crowds strung up sinners from telephone wires. They burned animals and children alive to appease ancient demons. They crucified all the lawyers of the nameless city. Of course, back then it had a name.

The city had been filled with lewd women with painted lips. Pious men would chain each limb of a woman to a different car, and then the vehicles would each drive toward a different point of the compass. They thought that perhaps this would give direction to their future. But that future was lost in a haze of heat and toxic fumes.

"We have to take a vote on it," Jeb said. "All who think it was a sin for Jonah to eat without giving thanks must now say 'Aye.'"

A loud, hungry round of ayes echoed through the hall. Jeb did not bother to ask to hear nays.

A young boy in the crowd gasped and fell to the floor. Sarah, an emaciated woman with bleeding gums and many sores on her skin, rushed to his side and cradled his head in her lap. "My son is weak from hunger," she cried. "If we do not have some food soon, he will starve to death."

Desperate for something—anything—with which to nourish her child, the woman picked a few large scabs off of her arm and pushed these into her son's mouth. The boy chewed gratefully.

Years passed, and many people took to living in cars. There was no gasoline left, but they still loved and took pride in their vehicles.

All the cars in town were rolled toward the casino-hotel-churches. People weren't allowed to live in these holy realms—they were a place for the purging of iniquities. Of course, that was before they realized the true value of sin.

The cars were nice little homes. To keep warm, they buried them in the sand. They took out the engines to make more room. Families huddled in their cars, in the cozy darkness. It became traditional to fasten the baby's cradle in place on the dashboard, so the wee one could reach up and play with the fuzzy dice hanging from the rearview mirror. From this choice location within the car, the baby could also be entertained by watching the insects and vermin that crawled on the other side of the front windshield.

"It is agreed upon. Jonah did sin by not giving thanks for his morsel. That leaves the count at one-thousand, nine-hundred and ninety-eight," Jeb handed Jonah a green token. "Is there any other sin I should record?"

The group was quiet. One could not make up a sin—for that they would cut out one's tongue, and fill the offending mouth with hot coals. There was words about that in all those old Bibles—"a tongue for a tongue"? Something like that.

"I had indecent thoughts about Jezebel," Matthew said. "I thought how delightful it would be to fornicate with her for long hours, well into the night."

"Yes, that is a sin," Jeb said, writing it down quickly and handing Matthew a gold token. "That is sin one-thousand, nine-hundred and ninety-nine. Any more?"

In the old days, back when there was power and cars were used for transportation, people paid good money to sin.

They watched half-naked women prance upon lighted stages. People use to gamble all night and all day. They danced, they gorged, they fought, they swore. There was even a whorehouse on the outskirts of town. The brothel did not operate in secret—it was an acknowledged business, and the employees even counted their purchases of sex toys and prophylactics as business expenses.

The country went up in smoke because they didn't watch their sins.

During the crazy times, they were less efficient when it came to dealing with sin. At times they even wasted precious foodstuffs. Some sinners would be covered in honey and then buried up to their necks in sand. They would then let armies of red ants chew them alive. Thus would they gnaw away the sins of the world. These tiny, industrious insects were the first sin-eaters.

But not the last.

When the Bibles were burned, one page—from the Book of Mark—had been caught by the wind and blown free. And this page told them a tale of wisdom. It told them all about Legion, a demon who was in fact a collective of evil spirits. Eventually they learned how to apply this wisdom to their lives, so that they might survive.

Jeb ignored the hungry growls of the crowd. "If no more sins are recorded, we must wait until the next Sunday when we meet."

"But I can't wait anymore," Eve said. "I must eat—I must! Please let us finish this."

"I only follow the rules," Jeb said. "My task is to count the sins. And since there are no more to count, I must conclude—"

"I pleasured myself," Moses blurted out. "Just before the meeting. My hand is still slick with my seed."

The room was quiet.

Jeb smiled for the first time all day. "Thank you. That is indeed a sin." He handed Moses a silver token. "We now officially have two-thousand."

Robed acolytes came forth out of the shadows with slender golden posts on wheeled bases. They arranged these in a pattern throughout the Great Hall. Then they connected the posts with purple velvet robes, creating a long maze that looped around the sacred craps table.

"Everyone who has sinned, line up in the order of the number on your token. Everyone else, please step aside," Jeb said.

After everyone had lined up, the acolytes came forth with buckets filled with ashes. They used the ash to write everyone's numbers on their foreheads. Then they collected the tokens and piled them up on the crap table.

Jeb then closed his eyes, thrust his hand into the pile and grabbed a token.

The people in the velvet-roped line-up stared at Jeb with fearful eyes. And yet they also began to wipe drool from their eager mouths.

Jeb looked at the token he had selected. "Number one-hundred and thirty-eight." He looked in the Sin Book. "Here it is. 'Adam drank alcohol until he became ill.' Yes, he will do. Adam, step forward."

Adam was a short, bald man who was now sweating heavily.

"Please wait here," Jeb said.

Jeb's boss made him nervous. This privileged individual was the only person allowed to live in the casino-hotel-church. He lived alone in a high suite—nobody was allowed to go up except Jeb, after the count.

Jeb climbed the stairs, up and up and up.

The crowd waited.

Eventually Jeb's boss followed his minion back to the hall.

The people, as always, gasped when they saw the boss. His was an appearance to which one could never become accustomed. His skin was as orange as the sun, and his slit-pupil eyes were bright green. His lips were bright red and his hair was long and black. He wore no clothes but carried a burlap sack.

He looked strange, yet in their sun-baked desert world, he didn't look out of place. In fact, he resembled a desert snake.

He was Legion, and he was many.

The people of the city without a name had given much discussion to Legion, for his page was all they had left of the Bible. Their thoughts drew him to them, and when he arrived, he struck a new bargain with them. A whole new *system* of vice management.

"Two-thousand sins . . . " the demon hissed, with a voice like a whispering congregation of evil. "A feast of sin for me. And now, a feast for you."

Legion stared at Adam intently. The bald man began to swell, and he hunched over until at last he had to drop to all fours. Bristles popped out of his pink flesh, which was becoming thick and leathery. His neck bulged out, his eyes sank inward and his nose lengthened into a quivering snout.

The people of the nameless city brought out ropes and soon they had the fat hog hanging by its hindlegs from a beam above one of the stages. Legion pulled two objects from his sack. He stuck an apple in the pig's mouth, and then handed a butcher knife to Eve and allowed her to slit the beast's throat.

"Again you have saved us," she said.

The green-eyed sin-eater smiled and looked out over the Great Hall, at the sun-scorched, hunger-maddened masses. So many to share so little ... Some would not eat at all. In the end, most would only get a scrap of meat—enough to keep them alive and desperate in this casino Hell of their own making.

"Yes," he said. "You are lucky to have me."

Mike: *The origins of "Of Gargoyles And Sin" came from a short-short story I wrote called "The Sineater" (which was suppose to be published in the late, great Frightmares). It was about a sineater brooding on the top of a church that was soon to be demolished. I sent that nugget of a story and some ideas I had to Teri Jacobs. She was suppose to send it back after she finished her installment, but she kept developing the story and it kept getting bigger and bigger. She had finished the story on her own. She did an excellent job of turning the yarn into a beautifully written epic dark fantasy.*

Teri: *I thanked Mike for allowing me to work on his idea. At first, we intended to share the writing, but the idea completely obsessed me and I begged Mike to let me run and play with his "baby." "Of Gargoyles And Sin" is one of my favorite stories, gothic and fanciful, with a brilliant theme (thanks to Mike!!!).*

OF GARGOYLES AND SIN

Teri A. Jacobs and Michael McCarty

They would spawn in the spoils of the soul.

But first Hakon must find her in the sin-infested, septic, sapropelic ruins of Paris, in the bowels of loathsome places where phlegmatics gather in swarms and pollute the air with disease-dirty breath, where the hideous press their rankled flesh against the lost children and whisper viscid secrets in their ears, where copious screams of the abused and damned echo unheard by the unfeeling. Her kingdom come.

No matter her disguise, he would know her by her burning sulphur musk. Stolen flesh could not dampen her scent, and he would find her, to have her.

Hakon shifted his stony face, glanced down from his perch at the cathedral's ground lights which glittered like fallen halos, and leapt from his heights, keeping to the shadows. Wind beneath his broad, leathery wings carried the chaotic songs of sins, broken harmonies of broken souls. As the wind thrummed against him, the iniquitous music wafted on his ear and drifted into his dead-gray flesh. Vile rhythms hummed through his bloodless veins, sputtering his heart into thunderous hungry rapping, and he honed in on the violin-screech of a recent transgressor.

He was a sin-eater, and he would feast tonight.

Sirens wrestled with the sinner's shrilling notes, ugly sounds grappling with one another as if they were part of a switchblade symphony, of operatic screams, steel drums, and blood ringing out like Angelus bells. The sins tolled louder in death, much louder than the sirens coming for the dead.

And Hakon harkened to its devotional call.

Darker than the night, clouds of smoke rose from the burning house and billowed across the sky, choking him with memories of that wretched war and the gluttony which destroyed his kind. Too many dead scattered across the country; too many sins to gorge upon. Cathedrals, churches, and courts had fallen, and its gargoyles, fat with the black plague of human sin, had perished.

As Hakon flew through old gold flames, he remembered *her* on the battle fields, charnel-carnal writhing with her lily white thighs clasped around the charred hips of a disemboweled corpse. She was in visceral love. Mouth smeared with the dead's sallow grease, she had grinned at Hakon, disengorged herself from the stiff corpse, and beckoned him with her red clotted tongue, a long tendril that reached to her fiery vulva and licked those burning lips of Hell.

Flurries of dust, smoke, and ashes of death had descended upon her, and, by the time he had reached her in the midst of destruction, all that remained was her echoic laughter.

A hundred years gone by, and Hakon walked through ashen air again.

The stench of scorched flesh greeted him as he worked his way deeper into the building, and, though the blackish haze obscured his sight, the peals of horrid sin led him back through tunnels of hallways and down into the labyrinthal collapse of construction supports, plaster, and wood. Beneath the crackle of fire and pop of bubbling skins, a whisper of purity whistled. An innocent soul, infantile in the ways of sin. He stopped, stooped, and swayed to its sound, a delicate lute played as with angelic fingers, the hymns of the morning as the sun rose in glory. The song which through the centuries lulled him to sleep.

The child, a blackened mass, was tangled in the arms of his mother, and the absurd sculpture of their melted skins and melded bones steamed and hissed. Something about the child's gaping, scorified mouth hinted of agony and terror and confusion. Hakon felt its heat, like intense screams, rise off the child. Heat to combat the icy grasp around him, his mother's arms pinning him to his death.

With his talons, he peeled off the mother's face. Waxy puddles of her eyes stared, and he dug into her sockets, emptying her memories into his gnarled palm.

. . . *drug euphoria, scalpel dreams, and a slick newborn placed in her arms, its weak mewling disturbing, coming from that tiny mouth on that tiny head. Too tiny for its plump body . . .*

. . . *headhunter victim walking, shrunken head toddling, face of wide eyes smiling stupid, can't see the disgusted stares . . .*

. . . *microcephalic child in a macrocosmic world, and she cried every night, red eyes and heart swollen with hate and anger, her perfect womb for deformity slashed with the razor . . .*

. . . *acid in her contacts, burn his sickening-defective image from her mind, but he won't go away from her nightmarish life, awash in the gasoline bath, and she struck the match to end her own self pity . . .*

Hakon removed his talons from her empty pits.

Poised above her chest, he sniffed her murderous sin, of pustulating wounds and oddly of black licorice, and his mucoidal spit dripped onto her tar-sticky flesh, sizzling. Hakon snapped his lithic fangs upon her. The flesh rippled as though her skin and bones had liquified, waves of putrence flowing, her sins oozing bloated filth and filling his gargoylian mouth with liverish tumors.

His mouth vibrated with her symphonic sins.

High madrigalesque songs drilled into his teeth, through the gums, roots and shrieking nerves, and into his brain where every ganglion mass exploded with sensory overload. Deep in his cortex, pleasure and pain quivered like violent-plucked harp strings.

Oh, the lyrical sins, his mind sighed. *Sins like the Greek Sirens, insidious-voiced creatures, luring him to death with the sweet-songs.* Even if he encountered heaps of those who met doom before him, he would carry on through that sea, enraptured, captured by the flutes of human gracelessness.

And so his visions swam into the mythic.

Real world vanished, Hakon drifted in a white sea, its pearlesque waters sweet as mother's milk but cold as death. Dark amorphous shapes floated in the deep, releasing gases, hollow ballads, into the sulking sea. This was her soul, this sea. Fluid, shapeless, life-giving, life-taking, beautifully alien and harboring dangers.

He dove into her depths and gnashed into the black-squid evils. Squealing songs were emitted, and then a gurgling quiet after he devoured the last of her squamous sins.

In the pure white sea, her soul emptied and redeemed, Hakon drifted satiated for the moment and listened to the distant sirens of the damned calling him.

Water blasted and pelted him from his phantasm as firemen hosed the flames.

Crawling through the detriment, he returned to the night air of smoke and chill and watched the firefighters from the heights of a neighboring building. He was shaken from his sin-opiate experience. Each feeding brought him closer to his end, the way he slipped into illusions, the sign of his mind crumbling into the dust which he would become. The stone of his flesh weathered finally by time.

As the blaze dwindled to embers and the singing sins dissipated into smoky murmurs, Hakon found himself furious at the men in their yellow slickers and olive-black boots, how they thought themselves noble and valiant, with their grim pride melodious in their hearts, them tone-deaf to their sins. How he wished he wasn't aware of the somber state of his soul. Nor of his aching loneliness.

Only a handful of his kind left in the world, guarding different corners of the earth, hoarding their lots of sin, never meeting another, and *her* teasing him through the centuries. The myriad of faces she'd worn; the number of seductions she'd sworn his way. His desire, the chains that weighed on him.

But he had no wish to be free.

Winds mimicked her sulphurous perfumes, and he didn't fight the euphoria simmering in his loins. How close he'd come to having her then . . .

. . . when she had climbed his spire, claws clinging to the bricks, scraping and scaling her way toward him. She had emerged with a terrible face, bright lotus eyes blooming with zeal, black skull showing in the cracks of the withered skin, and, when he had asked her name, she had grinned and ripped out her tongue. Standing before him with the serpentine tongue squirming in her hand, she had urinated at his feet. She had reached into the plum-bloody streams and wet his mouth with her salty, primordial piss. He had tasted her fertility.

As he had clasped his teeth into her flesh, she had slithered away from him, laughing until her ribs struck out like adders from her cloak of human skins, so she had sloughed off the skins and discarded them at his feet. All of her gone but the reptilian shred of her true flesh in his mouth . . .

Beneath the stars and neon lights, Paris glowed a gilded city in the aged darkness, garish as its Opera House, and Hakon staggered in the lure of its hideous music. The tiles beneath his clawed feet shifted and threatened to spill him upon the pavement, amongst the tempting sinners. For the soul-sushi buffet below, his capacious hunger growled and viscous drool filled his mouth. He licked the dripping tar from his jaw, reeling in obese-madness. Black sins, pulpy and fat, sang in falsetto and anise-flavored allure, making him sway dangerous upon the roof's precipice.

But he mustn't feed again.

Lest he grew too corpulent to mate, and by morning he would perish without leaving his seed to further the legacy and man would suffer eternal damnation without a sin-eater to cleanse the soul. He would join man in Hell if he failed. Forever taunted with the symphony of sins blasting upon him with no mouth to feed.

Snarling, he snapped his jaws and whipped his head in shaky denial, tarry spit flying and steaming across his face and into his eyes. Hakon gave a guttural cry before he flew into the air with a great hollow hunger.

Mists rose from the Seine, its waters moving sluggish through the city. The swirling strands reached upward, disembodied lily limbs beckoning suicide-urchins from the bridge and clasping cemetery dreams onto their disturbed faces. Child lovers, he saw as he drew near. *Amour* blushed their delicate faces, tainting subtle masculine angles with dainty pale pinks, and the boys' lush lips parted with anguished breath and wanton-urgency as cerise tongues slid from their mouths and entwined in final farewells. The fair and frail stripped down to their pallid flesh, pressing sticky sores against one another in wet-pussy kisses.

The river wind-whispered, *come.*

Seraphim falling in celestial screams, the boys splashed into the shallow spume. Bodies broke upon the rocks; pubescent cocks spasmed as death orgasmed through them. Tiny waves lapped at their spills, swallowing their delicacy of raw oysters and cream with bubbling sighs.

Miasmic *chansons*, sweet as jasmine and rose, piped out of shattered skulls and fractured femurs, and Hakon tasted their syncopated sensual sins within the mist. Hovering above their corpus-mangle, he inhaled mist and mortal-musk. He breathed in euphonic vapors.

Caught in an osmotic feeding frenzy, gulping breath after achingly sweet breath, he choked and gagged on his tongue, but he found he couldn't stop and would rather swallow his tongue than give up this empty feast. He felt like a lotus-eater, floating in drugged indolence, as he ravished the boys' sins in this vicarious fashion. His mouth watered for the vanilla boys below. Imagining blood as chocolate and sperm as custard, dulcet desserts for a carnivore carnival, he dove acrobatic through the air. Sweet, sweet hideous sins, ambrosial raping his mind.

The mists deepened into fogs, into hazes of opium and poison, and he staggered euphoric and delirious to the sloshy ground. Ogrish fairies with moonlight wings banded upon the water. Hakon blinked as the fairies cast extra long shadows which writhed and hissed like serpents in the river, coiling blackness upon dead-boy prey, until the shadows wound into one stretch of a slender woman.

Kneeling in the moon glistened water, she gleamed in ebon brilliance. Her night-shine skin seemed oiled with charm as Hakon moved closer to her, or maybe it was the way she kissed the dead boy, chewing first into his lips and then into the meat of his mouth, french-kissing-tasting-eating tongue, cheeks, tonsils, which drew him near.

He crawled along the shore and sank into the mud, soft and yielding as the inside of flesh. The mud sucked at his feet and wings, mimicking the sounds of the wet feast in the river, and somehow Hakon found it erotic to think himself fodder for once.

And he found her loving the dead, necro-erotic.

She had kissed the grimacing flesh from the dead boy's face, leaving him skull-boned and bound with her lithe legs, and, with his skull grinning between her thighs, rubbed herself against the bone of his chin.

Awed, he watched her clit swell, plump as a livid grape, and burst in orgasm, spilling sanguineous wine into the boy's gaping jaws. The breeze was spiked with her pungent suffocating odor.

Hakon sipped her scent and swaggered lust-drunk onto his clawed feet. Peacock display of storm-gray wings and snarling song, he strutted toward her, but, as if she had known he watched her the entire time, she glanced his way and shook her head, denying him with a bright red grin. She leapt up from the dead boy and ran through the water away from him, splashing, giggling, challenging him to chase her through the barbed wire fence lining the shore.

As she slipped between the wires, the barbs hooked through her borrowed skins. Black satin ribbons of flesh streamed in her wake and fluttered in the snickering wind. Again, it was all that was left of her as she disappeared into the darkness, swift and silent as a cobra.

Hakon circled the perimeter of the fence, sniffing the air for a lingering scent trail of the elusive. He caught a whiff of rats and disease but not of her.

In the nearing streets, sin whistles and glass bottle serenades shattered the night's sleeping hush, and his stomach gurgled like the sewer for the human wastes. He changed his course and followed the maze of chaotic streets, wandering deeper into corrosion and filth. Trash and feces littered the sidewalks. In the shadowed doorways, rag-doll prostitutes hid their bruised and puffy faces behind a veil of cigarette smoke and advertised their cheap rate by their stink of sex.

Hakon slipped into a vacant building, its insides gutted by fire and thieves, and settled near the window. Wraiths flickered silver in the night sky as they made their way beyond the world, some mouths gaping silent screams, others whispering like the wind in despair, a tortured hush which flowed into his heart and depressed him. Sin-deprived, he rocked lethargic, hugging his hard frame with shaky limbs, reeling in the hallucinogenic perfume of nostalgia.

. . . *noxious gases surrounded the spinning stars as he floated in the cold black of space. Light collided with light, and these fumes exploded into the churning ether, turning him inside out, remaking him into something else. His first memory before he woke in the world. His second, of the womb which expelled him, black as the space from which he came and as cold, that hole hissing with the noise of a thousand snakes, his umbilical cord whipping and tangling with the million others she had birthed. Then his mother, Lilith the first mother of man, gave him her soul to suckle, her sins echoing in the static music of the stars. He slept for a thousand years, drugged by her taste and scent of sulphur . . .*

A tincture of dawn crept into the darkness, and the bluing horizon brought Hakon to his senses.

Below a heroin addict dozed in a puddle of piss, the needle in his thigh looking like a plastic erection. Small dogs roamed around his body, sniffing, adding timid squirts to the mix, but the pack scattered when someone rounded the corner. Sulphur masked the urine.

Beneath a gas lamp, *she* stood dimly lit, the cowl of her new skins glimmering crimson. She pulled the hood of human flesh back, revealing cadaverous eyes, and sighted him in the rafters. They stared at one another like wolves in the shadows before their prey.

In the distance, Notre Dame rang its bells for early mass, and the clangor of brass and falsetto sins waking lulled Hakon into a drowsy stupor. Her wet-gore visage faded in and out of his waning sight. Eternal sleep weighed upon his granite lids, crumbling tears of dust from his eyes, and Hakon struggled against the harrowing darkness which awaited him.

He leapt from the rafters and landed upon the decrepit floors, clouds of grit rising and choking him as much as the blood-reeking smoke of the old war. He trudged through the building, reeling in hunger wounds, toward the battle grounds of propagation.

Tyranny in her eyes as he approached, but she remained beside the lamp, awash in jaundiced light, her ancient sins trumpeting, her red vulval mouth gaping in a hideous grin.

Coy, golden-cyclopic god, the sun, winked above the horizon, scintillating rays conducting the cherubim, cupid bow lips upon phallic flutes. Dawn songs tearing him apart from the inside, the stone of his flesh cracked.

The world would not stand still, no matter how much he longed for this moment, longed to savor her, and Hakon gripped her with his lithic fangs. She succumbed to his fierce embrace. Ardor-clasped in his mouth, her flesh softened, transmogrifying into the ethereal, and he bedded her in the soul of the addict.

Operetta of iniquity performed as he fed off the addict's soul. Engorged, he turned upon her. He had his claws torn through her, holding her in the tumultuous dance, their amorphous bodies tumbling upon each other, twisting, fighting, mating like brutal sharks with teeth serrating and male-claspers piercing unyielding holes in this black sea of the addict.

Hakon sighed a final breath with his final thrust, shuddering in pain and orgasm, releasing her unto the bright world. The black sea carried him under, into its cold depths, and he drifted toward death, utterly exhausted and wasted, yet with hunger abated and calmed by the melodious sound of her belly bubbling with an embryo of a sin-eater.

Mike: *Ron and I used to play together in the acoustic group Carnival Of Souls — which was more an excuse to get together to play guitar, drink beer and laugh all evening. One night after practice we were discussing the fact that protagonists in most science-fiction stories are portrayed as heroes. After a few beers more I told him about my idea of a loser scientist. Ron loved the premise and we started work that night. "Sugar Daddy" has been read at conventions, bookstores and even on the radio. It is one of my personal favorites.*

Ron: *I thought the idea of a loser scientist who creates a perfect woman was sad and hilarious at the same time. Our friends and family look at us as slightly off-kilter and this is the kind of story we love to play with. I remember growing up watching old horror and sci fi flicks at his house and we'd be alternately scared and amused at each one.*

SUGAR DADDY

Michael McCarty and R.L. Fox

I only wanted love — is that so wrong? Wanting love? Desiring companionship?

I was a winner at science and a loser at love. In love I had zero, zilch, nada. In science, I had won a Nobel and was the top scientist in the world in the field of Micro-Genetics Engineering.

I couldn't help the fact that I was ugly as a toad. If chicks dug brains — my date card would be constantly filled. If only I had washboard abs, instead of this washing machine gut.

One day while watching a porno, I came up with a marvelous hypothesis. Since I had failed miserably, numerous times, wooing women, maybe I should just create one.

The plan was so simple that it was brilliant. I'd combine old-fashioned robotics with state-of-the-art circuitry, hydraulics and plastics to create the woman of my dreams from scratch.

I immediately surfed the net — searching all the obvious places;

A.I. research, cosmetic reconstruction, silicone enhancements and my favorite X-rated sites. I quickly downloaded and started analyzing all the information.

Shifting through all these facts, my mind started to wander and I thought about my past first love and how fate intervened . . .

I almost lost my lunch when I looked up and noticed Fiona Carmichael's eyes on me. I couldn't believe one of the most attractive women at Princeton would cast her baby blues in my direction; not only that, but they were actually staring at me.

She even spoke. "I noticed you."

My heart almost stopped. I could hardly breathe. "Huhhh-what?"

"I noticed you in class today," she said. "When you told Professor Forsyth about his lack of, what did you call it—his lack of prowess in the electro-chemical field?"

Professor Forsyth oversaw a tough curriculum and was notorious for being harsh and unforgiving with his grading curve.

The love affair lasted as long as the class did. When the semester was over, so was the romance. And when I tried to pursue her during the summer, she said those vengeful words that still tear my heart apart:

"Making love to you was like doing it with the Pillsbury Dough Boy."

The only good from all of this was it led me further down the path of science; where everything made sense. Women didn't love me, science did.

With my Internet connections and my Visa Platinum, the deliveries started to arrive at my door daily. Every time I opened a package, I saw yet another piece to my creation taking shape. I felt like Hugh Hefner meets Doctor Frankenstein.

I assembled all the various parts, gadgets and gizmo; even created some of my own. In no time she was fully assembled. A completely operation android. And the eerie thing was . . . she was a dead ringer for Fiona. So I named her Fiona Two.

In this day and age, you're not supposed to achieve love through mechanical means, but I was all too eager to make love to

Fiona Two immediately. Regrettably, in that department she was too much like Fiona One.

I tried all the conventional dating techniques: movies and music, candles and dinners, flowers and begging—nothing worked.

Defeated, I sat down at my lab table and was reviewing my notes. I took out a candy bar, unwrapped it and was going to take a bite when Fiona Two suddenly leaped on my lap and stared at the Snickers with lustful desire.

Women equate chocolate with love, so it didn't surprise me very much that a robotic woman would do the same thing.

I ran down to the convenience store and stocked up on all their candy.

As long as there were sugar products in the house the loving didn't stop. But I got tired of constantly hitting the candy venders—it left me no time to dabble in science. That was when I decided to invest in a vending machine.

The vending machine was the best of both worlds: it gave me some much-needed time to do experiments and kept my robo-girlfriend in her sugar fix. I even gave the machine a voice so that it could announce when supplies were running low.

Even though I kept the candy supply well-stocked, the loving started to slow down. I suspected an affair, but I had no idea of who on Earth she could be cheating with, because her existence was a secret.

Then one day after working long hours in the lab, I discovered the painful truth. I walked into the bedroom and to my horror I saw Fiona Two's mouth all covered with melted chocolate. She was yanking the levers over and over and the vending machine, that damned two-timing machine, kept saying, "Who's your daddy? Who's your daddy?"

Mike: *This was the first story that Teri and I wrote together and it is my favorite collaboration. This story was written over the internet, sending the story back and forth over several weeks. I felt like a tightrope-walker without a net because I didn't know which direction Teri was going to take me. The story is dark, creepy and even a little sexy. I wasn't surprised about a year later to learn she'd write her debut novel The Void (which I wrote a blurb for) because this lady has talent.*

Teri: *Mike took my collaborating virginity with this story. Aptly, "Skull Job" involves some deviant, nasty scenes that only two people can do. Mike directed the plot and I fleshed out the scenes with details. The experience couldn't have been more fun! And I still love the twisted ending.*

SKULL JOB

Teri A. Jacobs and Michael McCarty

My dick had gotten me in trouble again.

I couldn't believe the predicament I was in, briefs stripped my ankles, hands behind my back in cuffs, blindfolded. But the smell was the worst thing . . .

The evening had started out promising. I had met this attractive young woman at the club.

She was dancing her booty—and what a hot booty it was, snug in her leather pants—off all night. Best of all, she was clearly flirting with me, smiling at me as she grinded to the beat. Her enormous breasts bounced with an opposing rhythm, but her long dark reddish hair kept cascading over them, obscuring my view of her peek-a-boo nipples through her sheer top.

When finally she went to the bar, I followed her. But, when I stepped up next to her, I couldn't think of anything to say. My mind went blank, and I blurted, "Hey."

"That your best line?" she asked.

I stammered with a dorky comment about how great she looked on the dance floor, but the DJ announced last call and killed me lame.

As the bartender handed her a sloe-gin fizz, she brushed a hand against my stomach. I sucked in just a bit for good measure and smile. She traced her fingers upward until they lingered upon my neck, chills tingling down my spine with her cool touch, and she tiptoed to whisper in my ear, "You look like you'd be interested in a skull-fuck."

"A what?" I said. With the loud music, I wasn't sure of everything she said except "fuck"—that my brain was trained to hear under any circumstance—all the while I slid my wedding band inside my jacket pocket.

"A skull-fuck," she said louder, taking off the sunglasses. One of her eyeballs was missing. And in the strobing light, in dry ice fog, she looked vampish—eerie, terrible, and mesmerizing. She led me to the back of the club where the music didn't blare and pulse from the speakers. "I want you to fuck my eye socket."

I was revolted and turned on that the same time. Her empty socket was of darkness and pink flesh, disturbingly similar to another hole, and while she waited for any response from me, she licked her glossy lips. I forgot about her eye as other, greater things popped into view of those breast heaving with her excited breath.

"I'm game for something new," I finally said.

"So you never fucked a skull before," she said. "Mmmmmm, I like virgins."

She pressed against me, her skin hot and sweaty, her breasts soft and yielding. With her head tilted up, she stared at me, and her one blue twinkled like an impish star. I jumped when her hand groped me through my jeans. I glanced around at the other Dungeon patrons, wondering if in their drunken haze they noticed this tasty vixen with the missing eye rubbing me hard.

"You'll fit fine," she drooled. "Maybe a little too thick."

My cock throbbed with happy ego.

"Do you want to leave?" I choked on my own words, still

tongue-tied around her.

"In a hurry to make me all 'cock-eyed'?" She laughed, and I chuckled along, beginning to feel more and ease with her and the idea of skull fucking. She enjoyed it, so it must be something good.

"Whatever you want." I placed my hand on the small of her back, pulling her closer to me, whispering in her ear. Her hair smelled of raspberries. On impulse, I nibbled her neck and tasted her sweet skin, wanting so much to lick her entire body. My cock strained against my jeans. Her fingers working up and down my shaft didn't help.

She kissed me then. Full on my mouth, her lips pressed with a sense of urgency that I couldn't respond to at first, only standing there feeling her kiss as though I were putting it to memory. Velvet petals crushed for keepsake between book pages. I don't know why that came to mind, maybe the violet taste of her mouth, the scarlet-stain of her lips. But then I forgot in the petals and opened my mouth, allowing her tongue entry. Her tongue circle mine, lazy at first, teasing. She moaned as she did this, and my mouth vibrated with her voice, a total passion titillating every nerve from my mouth to the core of my being.

Cupping her chin in my hand, I kissed her deeply then withdrew, a diamond-glittering strain of saliva connecting us still.

"Let's go now," I breathed heavily.

Exiting the club quickly, her leading me with swaying hips, we made it to the parking lot. The reek of the dumpster accosted me, and only one street lamp illuminated the oily darkness. Standing beneath it, she was awash in the saffron glow. Creepy the way she looked at me, her one eye like a dim star, the other a black hole.

She unlocked her car with a press of a button, and it chirped as though it were one of the night's insects singing for its mate. I slipped inside its dark interior, feeling apprehensive as if I had just entered a cocoon. Something about the way she clicked her teeth put me on edge, but my fears fluttered away as she leaned over from the driver's side and unzipped my pants.

"A little something to keep you interested," she said fondling my rigid cock, bringing it out from its denim confines.

With a wide grin, she lowered her head upon my lap. She tilted her head to the side so that I could watch, and I held my breath as her mouth neared and formed an "O." Warmth of her breath against me, then the heat of her mouth engulfing me. I shifted my hips a bit, wanting her to take the entire length in, but she stayed at the head, licking around it, toying with the scar of my foreskin cut. The old lollipop song filled my mind, made me smile. Then she swallowed the whole sucker. Gripping the shaft, she worked her hand up and down while she bobbed her head, her mouth the perfect blend of tightness and wetness and flickering tongue along the bulging vein. The expert way she sucked made me realize I wouldn't take too many licks to get to the creamy center.

I groaned my chuckle.

Then she stopped.

"I can't wait to have you inside me," she whispered.

I nodded, waiting for her to put her mouth deliciously on my cock again, or undress and spread those well-toned legs of hers, or anything like that. But all she did was start the car.

I tucked myself back in, wiped the sweat from my forehead, and sank into the leather-bucket of her Mercedes-Benz, too aware of the vibrating rumble of the engine in my seat, of the humming memory-echo of her mouth.

As she drove from the safe confines of the downtown district, she rattled on. Speeding through her ramrod history—her name, Selena, daughter of a Cuban singer and German scientist; worked as an arts dealer in Soho; shacked up with an ophthalmologist boyfriend, Leon; artist friend designed a glass eye for her—the golden eye of Horace—until she found a suitable replacement.

She stared at me as she said this, dissecting my face, my eyes. Her mouth widened.

Clubbing every Monday and Wednesday nights at the gothic clubs, she said, made her feel less like a freak.

"Do you mind if I ask you a question?" I asked.

"Shoot, go ahead, ask me anything." She smiled.

"How did you lose your eye?"

She fell silent. An unsettled quiet, with only the deep rumble of the engine and the whine of the tires, like some hungry beast prowling the streets.

"Sorry, didn't mean to pry . . . "

"Pry," she laughed, harsh, bitter, the sound as twisted as her mouth. "Exactly how I lost my eye."

Screwdriver wedged into socket, metal against bone, metal against soft blood-swollen orb, pulling, pushing, prying . . .

Popping . . .

Sickened by my imaginings, I turned from her, looked out the window, and wondered if I could really fuck that violated hole.

But then I though of strong hands—mine—pinning her down, ripping away her clothes, thrusting fingers in her unwilling cunt, making her scream . . . and I knew I could.

Soon the glitter of the downtown buildings gave way to dark, deteriorating warehouses, abandoned row houses, and rusted train yards. The number of street lights dwindled, and the night crawled along side the car as she drove deeper into a forgotten section of town. She pulled into a parking lot next to a dilapidated brick building. When she killed the cars lights, the shadows strayed from their corners and gathered in the open, and, since I wasn't used to a non-suburban setting, I imagined the red eyes of the rats were really demons waiting to steal my soul.

Selena ran her warm fingers along my bare arm and linked them with mine, bringing both our hands up to her chest. Beneath the black mesh, her nipples stood erect.

"Ready?" she asked with a giggle. With her other hand, she reached over and groped me. "Yes, I feel you are."

Giggling like a high school girl making behind the bleachers, she got out of the car, and I followed her like a horny schoolboy into the dreary apartment building.

Inside the apartment, I was struck by claustrophobic fear. The low ceiling and narrow hall pressed upon me, and the way the lights scattered from the broken bulb reminded me of translucent spider webs. With each step, I avoided the dim-lit strands, feeling ridiculous and scared of the tricks my mind was playing on me.

Strange noises, a myriad of soft clicking and scuttlings, echoed from the darkness ahead. I couldn't help but think of insects and traps and me as their prey.

I noticed a foul scent as well, but I couldn't place it, what with Selena stripping her top off and giving me an eyeful of her fleshly mounds, definitely more than a handful but never a waste as I licked my lips and walked to her.

She thrust her chest forward, erect nipples pointing to my cupped hands, and I took her breasts in my eager hands.

"Grab them rough," she said.

In my mind, I heard "go-ahead-take-me; make-me-bend." Something my wife never let me do—she always needed gentle touches and caresses, missionary that's taken me to the brink of madness. Here this stranger wanted me to be a little rough, allow the caveman in me to come out. Thousands of years of evolution hadn't wiped him out of my jeans.

I pushed her breasts together, licking her nipples, then sucking them hard. I bit beneath the bottom curve of her right breast, and she cried out, "Oh yes." Perfect as a porn star.

She fumbled with my snap and zipper and pulled my jeans down. With a grin, she squeezed her breasts together and lowered herself upon me. My cock slipped between her breasts.

"Want a titty-fuck?" And she worked her breasts up and down my long cock without waiting for me to answer.

Not that I would've said no.

As the head of my cock popped up from her breasts, she gave it a quick suck before it disappeared down again. I gasped and ached for more.

She released her breasts, and the snug-soft pressure of them was gone, but she continued to suck me, deep-throating me until I was all but lost inside her. With a slow retreat, Selena removed her mouth—*no, no, no,* my mind screaming, not wanting her to stop when I was so close. Then she rubbed my wet cock against her lips, her cheek, her eyelid. Her eye socket swallowed my cock.

Before I could register odd sensation, of bony ridges and soft insides, she quit.

"No skull-fucking yet. First, I want you to get me really wet," she teased, unbuttoning her red leather pants, hiding fingers inside.

I tugged them over her hips, and she stepped out of them and stood before me with only a thin black g-string that barely covered the V cleft between her muscular thighs. She toyed with her panties, moving the silk to the side, giving me a show of her pussy—pink lips, no whiskers. She dipped a finger between her lips, rubbing her swollen clit ever so slowly.

"As tight as a virgin," Selena said, parting herself for me.

Her pussy glistened with excitement, and I couldn't contain my own any longer. Dropping to my knees, I gripped her firm ass and pulled her close to my mouth. My tongue darted inside her, tasting deep, then up circling her clit, and she rocked her hips gently. I inserted a finger to match her rhythm.

"It feels so good. But I want to play a game before either of us comes." She pushed my head a way

"What kind of game?" I asked, relishing her flavor in my mouth.

"I Spy with a kinky twist." Smiling, she dangled a pair of police handcuffs before me.

"Sure," I'd drooled, spying plenty I wanted to fuck.

She cuffed me, then she tied a black blindfold over my eyes.

"But I can't see."

"I know. It's part of the game." Her voice skittered along the walls, and I worried she had left me alone, in the dark, vulnerable to whatever was unseen.

"Selena?"

Her small hand clasped my elbow as she led me down a flight of stairs. Cool, rank air rushed upon me. Shivering in the draft, I finally placed the smell, septic and sepulchral, like wartime fields stagnant with slaughter.

"There's a sofa over here." She pushed me on the couch and pulled mind briefs down. "I spy a big cock."

Something slick rubbed beneath my balls. Grinning, I shifted and allowed her better access to them, knowing it would be a hundred years too soon before my wife never took my balls and her mouth.

From across the room, Selena said, "I spy my whip."

I gagged and yelled, moving my ass away faster than a cockroach into a crack.

"What the hell was that?"

But she didn't answer me. The sounds of her footsteps dwindled as she left the room and headed back up the stairs. Other sounds replaced her steps, the scurrying of insects with mandibles clicking and hard shell bodies rubbing. I screamed when feathery feelers tickled my ankle.

Acid burn up from my stomach and into my throat, and I kept swallowing spit to keep everything down. The stench, the darkness, the creepy noise were tearing me apart from the inside. With deep breaths, I tried to stay calm and in control. My alcohol-heady exhale only added to the toxic air.

"Selena? Hey, we can stop with the games!"

Static of silence.

Bitch, I thought. *She's up there getting her kicks from watching me squirm.* Anger soon replaced my fear, and I made my mind to get up from this stinking couch.

"You're not leaving, are you? Not before the fun," she said with a husky voice as she traipsed down the stairs.

"This isn't my kind of fun," I replied.

"I forgot some toys though." Her lips were against my ear, and her candy-breath warmed me like hot cinnamon. She was just one of those girls that exuded sex. Sex I wanted bad enough to deal with some shit to get.

Soft amber light peeked through the blindfold. Selena lifted the blindfold off one eye.

"I spy a blue eye." Her plump lips stretched into an awful smile as she cuffed my ankles. "Maybe I'll get lucky tonight—it looks like the right shade this time."

Awful toys glittered in her bag.

But behind her, movement stole my attention. Cockroaches by the hundreds. Dark swarms crawling toward darker forms . . . corpses . . . all male, all missing one eye.

Selena put the blindfold back in place, and I sat still with shock, locked in cuffs, stripped of my jockeys, blindfolded, listening to the clink of her toys—the scalpels I spied in her bag.

Mike: *This is the first collaboration that Mark and I wrote together and it is also my favorite of our stories so far.* Mark approached me with the idea of writing a story for Warfear: A Collection Of Strange War Tales, *a hardcover anthology from Marietta Publishing. I had an idea brewing in my head that turned out to be perfect for a military story. Several years earlier, I'd read an article stating that millions of dust mites lived in the average person's bed, feasting on their dead skin cells. That seemed like a pretty disturbing notion, and so the story was born.*

Mark: *I've always enjoyed writing about insects. They're fascinating: tiny living creatures with no bones, and many have hard exteriors and an alien, mechanical appearance. With those thoughts in mind, I found Mike's story idea to be ideal material for a military story. Bugs certainly look like little war machines. Maybe Mike and I should write a story about army ants someday.*

MILITARY MITE

Michael McCarty and Mark McLaughlin

Once upon a time, the industrial military sector had complete economic and political control of the United States. But after World War II, the Korean War, Viet Nam, and every other conflict, battle and scuffle in our planet's various nooks and crannies, there came a day when folks just wanted to come home from work and log on to the internet.

People were bored with war. Besides, personal computers could play countless entertaining and harmless wargames—if a person felt like engaging in a bit of aggression, all they had to do was sit down in front of a monitor's comforting glow and begin to play.

The military had a hard time justifying bloated budgets to Congress. Congress still felt the need to protect America, but Army-wise, it was a time of penny-pinching policies.

The cuts soon followed. Bases and installations were shut down. Projects were terminated. Staffing was reduced. And Dr. Stanley Prince's name was at the top of several lists as a likely candidate to axe.

Prince, a thin, nervous man, was from the old school—more bureaucrat than mad scientist, involved in a number of pork belly science projects. He'd enjoyed some initial success in his career, but now, his colleagues simply couldn't remember the last time he'd presented an idea of royal proportions.

Prince sat in the crammed waiting room, flipping through a current issue of *Scientific American*, not really reading, just trying to look nonchalant. Actually, his heart was pounding like a conga drum.

"Mr. Prince," said the blonde receptionist. Her smile was just as artificial as her enormous bosom. "Major McQueen will see you now."

"*Doctor*," he said as he passed her desk. "That's *Dr.* Prince."

She smiled and shrugged.

W.W. McQueen was reading some papers when the doctor walked in. The major didn't make eye contact. He just pointed to the seat in front of his massive oak desk.

Prince sat in a small, velvet-cushioned chair. He stared out the window—the Major had a spectacular view of Washington D.C.

"Mr. Prince," the heavset military man said. "I have to cut over one thousand jobs this week alone."

"That's *Dr.* Prince," Stanley said.

The Major looked out the window. "Really? Where? I thought you were Prince."

Stanley smiled. "I was just pointing out that I like to be called Dr. Prince."

The Major cocked his head to one side. "Are you funning with me? I'm too busy for your fancy academic games. Like I always say, the only different between *aca*-day-mia and *maca*-damia is the letter 'm'. Other than that, they're both nuts."

"Not really, Major. You are mispronouncing academia to make the two words rhyme. And, macadamia doesn't have an 'e' in it."

The Major cocked his head to the other side. "Boy, the fun and games never stop with you, do they?" His furry white eyebrows lowered. "What I'm looking for is a reason why I should go to Congress and tell them the Pentagon isn't spending taxpayer money foolishly. I have been examining your records and frankly, I'm surprised that you haven't been in this Division Five office before now."

Stanley just nodded sadly.

"They call you 'a scientist's scientist.' Sounds like fancy double-talk to me. I have a note here that says you are, and I quote, 'A major think-tanker—someone with profound theories.' Pretty words, but we need results, not just speculation."

Stanley nodded again.

Major McQueen stabbed at plump finger at a printout. "In the heat of Viet Nam, you came up with this cockamamie proposal: performing voodoo rituals to bring dead soldiers back to life, cutting down on the number of new recruits."

"Nixon didn't have a problem with it," Stanley said. "But my superiors buried the project in mountains of paperwork and procedure. Even the undead cannot withstand red tape." He leaned closer to the desk. "An effective voodoo ritual can focus vast amounts of theta energy, so naturally—"

"What the hell is *theta* energy?" The major shouted, but he did not give Stanley time to answer. "Prince, that proposal wasn't science—it was bad science fiction. Like I said, I'm looking for results. I'm afraid I must recommend that you go into early retirement. You'll get all your pension benefits. Now sign these papers."

The scientist cleared his throat. "Major, this whole turn of events may be a little premature. I'm near a major breakthrough right now. My new project is going to produce this country's most destructive weapon since the A-bomb."

Major McQueen's eyebrows shut up. "Go on. You've got my attention."

"I have been working on Project DTD—that stands for Dust To Dust. I have been breeding special dust mites with enhanced abilities."

"*Dust mites?*" The Major stroked his chin. "They're really small, right? Can they carry around tiny microphones? How about laser beams?"

"Umm, no." The scientist said. He took off his glasses and rubbed the sides of his pointy nose. "Dust mites eat dead flesh. But I'm creating a new breed that consumes both dead and *living* flesh."

The Major nodded, a smile slowly stretching across his face.

Stanley put his glasses back on. "The possibilities are endless. Our planes could drop the microscopic parasites over an enemy's camp. Or, we could have another country sell them provisions loaded with our tiny friends. This new breed can survive in an aquatic environment, so we could even put them in an enemy water supply."

"Intriguing," the Major said. "Killer insects, but *tiny*. Much better than those killer cockroaches we were working on. Those things were as big as puppies—couldn't sneak 'em over enemy lines. So what's the hold-up?"

"The biggest problem I have is this: after the dust mites eat a substantial amount of flesh, they won't eat again for another forty-eight hours. They instantly become lethargic, sleepy—then, when they perk up again, they lay their egg clusters. First, I have to alter their reproductive cycle, since those prolonged rest periods will lessen their military effectiveness. Then I have to speed up their metabolism, to create a lean, mean, *constantly eating* war machine."

"Remember, Prince, I need hard proof. I can't show the budget boys a bunch of flim-flam."

Stanley nodded. "I understand. Give me another month and come to my lab in Nevada. If you don't like what you see, I'll sign your papers."

The officer thought about it for a moment. "One month, and one month only. And fix that bug problem! Find out how to wake up those little sleeping beauties of yours!"

In the next month, rebels in the tiny republic of Vreplakia tried to take over the internet. Their new flag featured a burning computer, surrounded by a phrase which translated in English to "What Will The Fat Americans Do Now?"

The efforts of Vreplakian hackers ruined e-commerce for countless U.S. businesses. This enraged Major McQueen, who said to his secretary in bed one night, "My God, that son of a bitch Prince better deliver the real deal. I'm itchin' to drop a planeload of those flesh-eating dust mites on those Vreplakian bastards. That'll teach 'em to mess with the red, white and blue."

The secretary smiled. "Their flag is red, white and blue, too. The flames are red, the computer is white—well, actually, more of an off-white—and the words are blue."

The Major gritted his teeth, but said nothing.

"Say," his bed partner continued, "if you're so worried about how that scientist is doing, why don't you just go have a look-see? You've got security clearance. You could do it at night, when he's asleep, so he doesn't think you're looking over his shoulder."

"You're not as stupid as you lead people to believe, are you?" the Major asked, impressed.

She shrugged. "Oh, what does a silly little Harvard valedictorian like me know?"

A week before his official scheduled visit, Major McQueen made a midnight stop at a Nevada lab. It was time to kick Vreplakian ass, whether Prince liked it or not. The Major also wanted to make sure this wasn't another of the scientist's crackpot schemes—if there was even one zombie involved, there'd be Hell to pay.

The lab was fairly spacious. In the center was a smaller room with plexiglas walls, containing five rows of tables. There were three aquariums on top of each table. The aquariums seemed to be in need of a good cleaning. They all seemed to have little clouds of lint floating around inside of them. Outside of the plexiglas room was a control module on a metal stand. The stand also held some weird-looking science instruments and a notebook.

The Major opened the notebook and flipped through the

pages. He saw dozens of crude drawings, along with some scribbled notes. He studied the pictures . . .

A piranha.

Foreign letters—probably Greek, since he recognized pi.

A preying mantis.

A black widow spider.

Roman numerals.

A razorback hog.

Some Egyptian hieroglyphics.

Laddery-looking spirals. Maybe it was that DNA stuff scientists liked to babble about.

He also found some sketches of naked ladies, along with some scribbled 900-number sex lines.

The Major had taken only a few science courses in college, but he could tell this was no scientific discipline he'd ever studied. This looked to him like . . . Like someone spending tax money as wildly as a drunken Hollywood hooker with a stolen credit card. Even worse, it looked like god-damned, son-of-a-bitchin' *science fiction.*

"*Failure,*" the Major hissed.

He tossed the notebook in the air and stormed out of the lab.

The notebook hit a button on the control module and a panel in one of the plexiglas walls slowly slid open.

In the morning, Dr. Prince was at work bright and early. Last night had been his first night out of the lab for nearly a month. He had a small cot and a dorm-style refrigerator in the back, since he was constantly working.

He opened the door, walked into the lab and saw his notebook sprawled on the control module.

"So much for security," he muttered. He'd had troubles with nosy guards in the past. That was why he wrote the most secretive aspects of his work in a special fluorescent dye—completely invisible unless it was held under black light. He smiled at a page of his crudely drawn naked ladies. The real secrets of Project DTD—including the formula for dust mite repellent—were written in his special invisible ink all over their bodies.

The doctor then noticed that the plexiglas panel was open. His smile turned into a grimace. He looked around, then realized that his special protective lab suit was in the back room, in a locker next to his cot. The dust mite repellent was in a sprayer—next to the suit. He turned to run, but it was too late.

The dust mites had found him.

His skin turned pink, then red, then bubbling maroon. His muscles actually *foamed* from the frantic activity, the microscopic *savagery* of the tiny creatures. His eyelids vanished, then his eyeballs burst and dribbled down his cheeks. His abdominal muscles foamed away and his intestines hit the floor with a wet, resounding *smack*. Even his bones dissolved into a gritty paste. Soon he was nothing more than a colorful pile of stinking garbage on the floor. But the wee monsters weren't done. Soon the reeking pile that had once been Dr. Prince was nothing more than a cloud of micro-shredded debris.

The entire process took the mites about three minutes.

Major McQueen, his immediate superior Lieutenant Colonel Troll and his ranking officer Colonel Wolf—all three were scheduled to meet with Dr. Prince at two o'clock sharp. They looked around the lab, waiting for the scientist. The place was a mess, with a big pile of dust next to the control module.

Impatient, the Major showed the other officers the notebook.

"I think Dr. Prince knew he had a failure here and left town," the Major said.

"I have to agree. Sad, really. And disgusting," Colonel Wolf said, staring at the pictures of naked ladies. He tore them out and crumpled them up. He tossed the paper onto the dust pile. "Get someone to clean up this mess," he said.

The major picked up the phone and called the maintenance department. A moment later, he walked out with the other officers. He tried to brush a streak of dust off of his sleeve, but he only succeeded in rubbing it into the fabric. He looked at Troll and Wolf. They too were streaked with dust.

Julia Blanca had been working in the Nevada Military Science Division for the last five weeks. The money was not too bad for mostly dumping trash. She had to take classes about bio-hazardous waste, but she kept falling asleep during the lectures. At any rate, it wasn't too bad a way to make a living. But working second shift, she didn't see her children until after the babysitter had tucked them in bed.

She swept up a mound of dust in preparation for loading it into a red plastic bag. But her wheeled work cart was out of trash bags. She tried to remember where the storage closet was, on this floor . . .

Then her pager buzzed. She looked at the displayed number. It was home. The kids again.

She sighed, then remembered the window in the hallway.

A minute later, she dumped the dust outside.

In the fresh air, the dust mites swirled along with the warm wind. They felt happy, sleepy and a little dopey, too, gorged on their recent meal—but soon enough, the egg-laying would begin. The wind carried them on and on, toward a magical kingdom called Las Vegas.

Mike: *Cindy has written several character sketches and one-act plays about a group of high school students during the '80s. I enjoy reading and hearing them—they're witty and well-written. One day I suggested that one of her dramas about teen suicide could be turned into a black comedy. I threw in a redneck character for laughs, since I really do enjoy the southern humor of Jeff Foxworthy, Etta May and of course, The Beverly Hillbillies. Cindy is a master of dialect, so she really helped to give the story an authentic accent. This is her first published piece of fiction.*

Cindy: *Michael and I were destined to collaborate on some project together since we both have an appreciation for dark comedy. We are also film buffs of cult cinema and B-movies—especially ones with an edge. We'd discussed writing a story along the lines of Better Off Dead, Heathers and The End. We hope we succeeded in creating something even a little wackier with "Hell's Bells."*

Although this is a satire, please don't try suicide at home.

HELL'S BELLS

Cindy Hulting & Michael McCarty

Deer Betty Lou:

U brok ma hart wen u left me 4 Billy Bob Buckallew. 4 da last 3 months I gives u all my luv, cash an' ma prize beer cans (even ma rare "Billy Beer" can ma grandpappy give me). I knows I'm beder lookin' than ol' Billy Bob cuz I has 2 times as manny teeth as that ol' buzerd. I evens got me one of dem dishus 4 da tee vee. Two bad I lost my shotgun when I went out coon huntin' with the boys—I reckon moonshine and coon huntin' don't mix—cuz I'd fil ol' Billy Bob ful of led.

Yas git the idea. By the time yas reed this note I wil bee pushin' up dayzees . . .

Luv,

Arlo Haywood Jr.

"Whew," he said, wiping the sweat from his forehead. "I'm plum tuckered out. Writin' that note was harder than the fourth grade." Arlo was speaking to his mangy mutt Buford, who was half blood-hound, half scurrilous cur, all wrinkles and flubber.

He put his pen down and walked into the bathroom, his old and faithful dirty dog lollygagging behind.

"I've heard that Jethro Dean Longenecker from Hogswart slit his wrists with a razor. Now the county have him locked up in some nuthut for tryin' to do himself in. I reckon I can do the job right, because that dufus screws up everythin' he does." Arlo paused and scratched his head and ass at the same time, mulling it over for a moment. "Yeah, that oughta be a good way to meet my Maker, don't ya think so, Buford?"

Buford responded by yawning and swatting a fly with his natty tail.

Arlo opened his medicine cabinet, searching for a razor blade. "Those city slickers always cut across. To do the job right, ya need to slice up and down—just like when ya gut a big ol' fish." He kept searching for his straight edge. "Damn, all I can find is my electric razor. Well that oughta get the job done faster, I s'pose."

He plugged in the shaver and it buzzed to life. He started shaving his left wrist when he heard a bell ringing. Arlo set the shaver aside and stormed off angrily toward the phone. "If it's some damn telemarketer I'm gonna raise some hell." He picked up the receiver, "'Yellow? Yellow?"

No answer but dead air.

He continued shaving his wrist for about another fifteen minutes.

"Maybe I just need to do it harder," he said and switched wrists, this time pushing the electric razor down with more might.

No cuts, no bleeding, just clean shaving.

"It don't work, dagnabbit. Boy, my wrists are as smooth as the bottom of a potbelly pig. Figures Jethro would come up with such a cockamamie notion. That is one strange boy."

Arlo pondered his self-destruction. He had no idea what to do next. "What do ya reckon I do to off mah-self, Buford?"

The dog was too busy licking himself to respond.

"I got it! Betty Lou always talked about that one poet lady, Sylvia Path or Platt or whatever her name was. My mind is like a damn fishnet these days, everything just keeps slipping through. That depressed lady who wrote all them depressing poems then killed herself by sticking her head in an oven. Sounds like a grand plan to me."

Arlo walked into the kitchen and Buford waddled after him.

The only oven that Arlo owned was a small microwave. He stuck his head inside. His curly red hair was streaked with grease since he hadn't cleaned up the possum stew he'd nuked the night before. He tried to close the door, but it kept hitting the back of his head every time he shut it.

"Ouch, damn blast, that smarts!"

Just then another bell started ringing.

"It better not be some dorky door-to-door salesman!"

Arlo pulled his head out of the microwave, ran to the door and threw it open. Nobody was there. "Probably some rug-rats playing ding-dong ditch. Heck, I use to play that mah-self when I was the runt of the litter."

He went back into the kitchen, stuck his head inside the microwave and repeatedly slammed the door shut on the back of his head. Finally he stopped. "My head is achin' somethin' fierce. There must be a simpler way to buy the farm."

Arlo sat down at the kitchen table and contemplated an idea. He thought and thought and thought . . .

"I gots it!" He snapped his fingers. "Ma great, great grandpappy once lynched a neighbor for cheatin' at cards. Hanged 'em up from the big oak tree out front. That would be a great place to string mah-self up at." He walked outside and Buford toddled along, following him to the woodshed.

"Damn blast it," Arlo muttered. "I'm all out of rope. I used it all up to bail hay last week." He looked around the shed. "Hmm . . . I still have some bungee cord left . . . "

He heard a bell ringing. He looked around but saw no ice cream truck. "Hittin' mah-self on the head might'a caused ma steel plate to vibrate."

He climbed up the tree, tied the cord to one of the sturdier branches and jumped off. Instead of breaking his neck, he bounced back up and hit his head on the same branch. The tree limb broke and fell with Arlo to the ground.

Defeated and disgusted, he gave up and laid on the dirt. Buford licked his face.

Suddenly he heard a rattling commotion. He sat up and saw a beat-up black pick-up truck with the words "The End" written on the side, pulling into his driveway. The driver was wearing black overalls, a red flannel shirt, cowboy boots, and on his head was a black hunting cap. He also wore dark sunglasses. In one hand he carried a pitchfork and in the other he carried two black cast-iron bells.

"Who's ya?" Arlo asked. "I never seen ya in these parts . . . "

"Ahm the Redneck Grim Reaper. Ya can calls me Grimmy, if ya like."

Confused, Arlo cocked his head to one side. "What's ya doin' here?"

"Look boy, jes give it up. It's over-time." Grimmy sighed. "Let me put it to ya this way — life is like a parkin' meter and yars ain't expired — ya still have a couple'a quarters left. I had to do in five fellers tonight and ahm tired. So give it a rest."

Neither one spoke.

Then Grimmy broke the silence. "Wait a minute . . . " He started ringing the bells. "Now it's gonna be six. But it still ain't yer turn — ya's too thick-headed to kill yerself."

"What's the bells fer?"

"These," Grimmy said, nodding toward the bells, "is hell's bells. Every time ya commit a cardinal sin or someone is gonna die, I ring the bell. Didn't ya pay attention in church?"

"Nope. Jes' plenty of shuteye during them sermons. Is them bells mentioned in the Good Book?"

Grimmy thought for a moment. "Maybe it got left out. I gave

the Editor ma notes, but I do recalls Him tellin' me he couldn't read my handwritin'."

If ya don't mind me askin'," Arlo said, "who's gonna buy the farm?"

"Billy Bob Buckallew. His heart is gonna stop while he's doin' the nasty with that Betty Lou. Now y'all behave yerself. I won't be seein' ya again fer a spell."

Grimmy walked back to his truck.

"Heya!" Arlo shouted. "Do ya mind if Buford and me hitch a ride with ya?"

"What fer?"

"My pickup is broken. Ya might have seen it by the pond, it's the one with the cement blocks instead of wheels."

"I knows that—it's dead, ain't it? I mean, what do ya need the ride fer?"

"Since yer goin' over to ol' Billy Bob's place anyway, I figures that Betty Lou's goin' to need herself a new man since her old one just croaked."

The Redneck Grim Reaper flashed him a smile. "Oh! Sure. Hop in, you two."

Arlo and Buford jumped into the truck. Grimmy started the truck and drove toward the horizon as the orange sun began to set.

Mike: *This was the first story written for Dark Duets. Ron was working on a dark fantasy novel called The Medallion. He asked me to take a look at it and give him some pointers. I liked it so much that I turned some of it into this short story. We were both influenced by "The Monkey's Paw" and this gave us a chance to put our spin on that classic tale.*

Ron: *Originally, the idea was to do a remake of W.W. Jacobs' "The Monkey's Paw" with our character being the last to own the cursed object. Mike collaborated to help condense the idea and create this story.*

THE WISHDOLL

R.L. Fox & Michael McCarty

Happy Hour was drawing to a close and I still wasn't happy.

I glanced up at the clock above the bar for the third time in fifteen minutes. I mentally cursed myself for still sitting here, waiting for my girlfriend, who I now was sure wasn't going to show. I drained my glass of beer, signaled for another and thought, "Screw her, why do I even bother anymore?"

I couldn't decide if I was more annoyed at Sarah for not showing up or at how stormy our relationship had become. We seldom talked to one another and when we did, it always ended in an argument. But we had agreed on a truce—to have a few drinks and laughs at Murph's.

I slid off the barstool, tipped the bartender and with glass in hand, I decided to wander over to the game room. I wasn't going to let her ruin my evening. The night was still young.

As I passed through the archway, I noticed a vintage Wurlitzer jukebox to my right. It looked like it must have been from the 1950s. To my left in the game room was a plate-glass window overlooking the street, with a wall of tables below it. The wall opposite the window had an electronic dartboard, a couple more tables and a door marked 'Employees Only' in red letters.

There was a young muscular man in a University of Iowa jacket and his girlfriend, decked out in the latest mall-fashions which clashed with her pierced eyebrow and lip. I could tell they had just started dating because of the playful taps and touches given in the happy/giggly way new lovers have. I tried to remember when Sarah and I were like that, but it seemed like eons ago. The fighting got in the way of the romance.

In the center of the room stood two pool tables, only one of which was in use. A white-haired man and a college student were finishing a game. The old man seemed to be winning easily, no luck here I guess. I wandered over to one of the low tables by the window and watched. The old man sunk the eight ball in a casual, well-oiled way, the kind of way you pick up after spending a life-time shooting pool in bars.

The older guy shook the student's hand and pocked a five. The kid strolled angrily out the back door.

"Up for a game?" I asked.

The old man looked up and said, "Sure, wanna put a five on it?"

"Nope, not after the way I saw you beat that last guy."

"How 'bout a beer then?"

"That I can do," I replied, as I put my quarters in the slot. After the ball finished rumbling down the rail, I racked them.

We introduced ourselves as we played. "I'm Cameron," I said. He said his name was Jack, and that he was "semi-retired and traveling around on a semi-working vacation." He said he'd been on I-80 heading east toward Chicago when his car started acting up, so he pulled into town to find a garage to have the car checked out. He had rented a car and a motel room, and decided to sightsee around the area. He liked the looks of this bar so he just dropped in for a few drinks before he called it a night.

I noticed he would glance from time to time at a small satchel lying against the wall near his stool, as if any minute it was going to do some kind of trick and he didn't want to miss it.

"That yours?" I asked, indicating the satchel with my cue-stick.

"Yup," he replied, waiting patiently. His eyes lit up as he said, "Some things are too valuable to keep lying around."

I should just have the word SUCKER tattooed on my forehead, I decided. I groaned inwardly and said, "Okay, I give up—what do you have?" I'm always looking for the angle, the con, in just about everyone I encountered.

He locked eyes with me for a few seconds, looked at the table, chalked his stick and said, "Tell you what—how would you like one of your wishes to come true? Anything you truly desired you could have—anything in the whole wide world."

"Yeah right," I said sarcastically.

"I'll show you what I mean."

Almost eagerly he knelt beside the case, spun it away from me, and released the catches. I sat down and waited while he dug around inside. Then he pulled out a little doll carved of wood and laid it on the table. "This is a Brazilian Wishdoll. I picked it up when I was in the French Quarter in New Orleans. It will grant you one wish—one wish only."

I had no idea of what he was babbling about.

"Take a look at it," he said.

I examined the doll. It looked a little like a tiki doll, but on closer inspection I noticed the colors were too vibrant, the face far too menacing to be some cheap carnival toy.

"It's ugly." I shuddered for no apparent reason.

"Yup, sure is. I know all this sounds like a lot of bullshit, but I'll tell ya what I'll do—we play best three of five, and if you win, I'll give you the wishdoll. Give it to you of my own free will."

"What if I lose three out of five?" I questioned.

"The loser of each game has to buy the next round," he replied.

I thought about this and figured at worst I'd be buying old man Jack three beers. At best, I'd win a few free suds with some cheeseball doorprize thrown in for good measure.

"I'm game." As we played, a recurring suspicion that I was in the process of being hustled kept coming to mind. I won the first game easily, a little too easily in light of my shooting.

He bought a round and we played another game. I was getting wary as I narrowly won the second game by a suspicious scratch by Jack on the eight ball. I figured he'd let me win a few, then boost the ante, set the hook and reel me in like a flopping carp.

I waited as Jack came back with some more beers. I took another look at the doll.

"Go ahead and touch it," he urged.

I tore my gaze away from the doll and looked up at Jack. He had little beads of sweat popping out of his forehead. My mental guard came up instantly, because this guy was scared, of what I wasn't sure, but he was definitely spooked by something.

Maybe he was afraid because he was within one game of losing that hideous doll, but that made no sense. Why would he want to further entice me by having me touch it and hold it in my hand? Unless, it suddenly struck, he was afraid I wouldn't want it—or worse, I'd lose the game and he'd have to keep it.

I once read a story in high school by W.W. Jacobs called "The Monkey's Paw." I looked at the doll once again and wondered if this object, too, held certain desirable properties but would doom the owner should it not be passed on to another before the owner's death.

This is silly, I thought—I'm just being paranoid.

Then I picked up the doll. I studied its eyes—they were made of some kind of stone, like tiger's eye but too maroon.

I felt a shock, a surge of energy that went through my whole body as if I had just touched a live wire. "What the fuck?" I dropped the doll back on the table, stunned. The couple across the room swiveled their heads in our direction, expecting some kind of confrontation.

Jack deftly swept the doll off the table out of view. It dropped back into his case with a thud of lost hope. He slid into the seat across from me.

I felt my head clear, and watched the couple resume playing darts, their voyeurism unfulfilled.

"What the hell was that?" I asked him.

"You felt the magic," he said in a hushed voice. "It is very powerful magic."

I had definitely felt something. My hands still stung. "If this thing really works, then why pawn it off in a pool bet?"

He took a sip of his beer before answering. "Sometime wishes can be dangerous."

Jack's point chilled me.

We started a new game, and as we played, it became apparently obvious Jack was intentionally losing. This made me more nervous. Jack left me with the eight-ball lined up—I popped the black ball into the side pocket easily. He re-opened the briefcase quickly and handed me the doll without a word.

The doll looked even more gruesome in my hands.

Jack finished his beer, said, "be careful of what you wish for"—and then left.

This was starting to spook me. I stuck the doll in my jacket pocket. I quickly finished the beer and ordered another. I had to figure out what to do. I thought about Sarah again. I was wondering what she was doing.

The loud country music and the alcohol made it hard to think straight. It was late and I'd had too much to drink. I was in desperate need of fresh air to help clear my mind.

As I carefully made my way home, I was still confused about the encounter with Jack, but I was also upset with Sarah for not meeting me as planned. What was even more disorienting was that I felt the doll move inside my pocket. I reached in, gingerly removed the doll and placed it on the passenger's seat. At the next stoplight I glanced down at it. Its eyes seemed to glitter with a malevolent glare. I quickly flipped it face down.

I made my way up the winding drive to our complex and noticed Sarah's jeep in our parking slot. My anger resurfaced as I climbed the stairs to our apartment.

She started in on me as soon as she heard me take my key out of the door.

"Where the hell have you been?" she called from the bedroom.

My head was throbbing and I was amazed to see the doll in my hand—I didn't remember picking it up.

"Where have you been?" I replied. "You were suppose to meet me at Murph's."

She entered the room. "After work I really didn't feel like going out, and I didn't think you would stay at the bar all night without me."

"Babe, I waited for you so we could talk," I said as I laid the doll on the dresser.

"Talk about what? Our non-existent sex life?"

My anger rose another notch, to the volatile and dangerous level.

"And why are you playing with dolls for God's sake?" she brayed. "Picked up some Girl Scout on your way home?"

"No, I—"

"I bet the Girlie Scout got you all hot and bothered, like the babysitter you kept eyeballing at your brother's house last week. Hey, better hop on before it starts to droop, like usual–"

Finally, I had enough. "I wish you'd just shut the fuck up!"

Normally she would have retaliated quickly, but as I gazed at her with mounting horror, I watched her lips grow together and seal up, until they were replaced with a solid wall of flesh.

Sarah was in hysterics. She rushed to the mirror, eye wide with horror, clawing at her own face. Falling to the floor, she writhed like an earthworm on a hot afternoon sidewalk.

Sarah would never speak again. She would never able to scream obscenities at me or mock my every move. I looked again at her as the tears streamed on her desperate face, and realized I would also never again hear her purr my name late at night—or the words, "I love you," whispered softly against my cheek.

Mike: *I've known Michael Romkey for years. I read all his vampire novels for a decade and they are among my favorite bloodsucker books. Since we both live in the Quad-Cities, we meet for lunch on occasion to discuss vampirism, the publishing business, music, etc. At one of these lunches, I off-handedly asked if he'd like to write a collaboration for Dark Duets and he surprised more by saying yes. This story was batted back and forth like a tennis match in hell until it the breathless conclusion. It was a challenging match, but a fun one.*

Mike R: *Writers often collaborate on scripts for movies and TV. I've always wondered how well that could work. I'm used to sitting alone, obsessing to a really foolish degree over things like how to describe the way a character walks into a room. I have to say I found this experience interesting. I banged out the first part of the story. McCarty added his part and sent it back via e-mail, going in a direction different from what I would have done. I tried to take the story off in a completely unexpected direction with my next turn, just to see how he'd respond. He hung with me. We should try this with a screenplay.*

BLOCKED

Michael McCarty & Michael Romkey

The little red light was blinking when Wheeler came back from the drugstore.

He knew it was going to happen. He had known it for months. There was no escaping it. The moment he signed his name to the elaborate document, accepting the proffered check, he had as good as sold his soul to the Devil.

And now the Devil wanted to collect his due.

The red message light on the answering machine winked balefully at him in the darkness.

On, off.

On, off.

They were relentless!

Wheeler sat down at the kitchen table, pushing the empty coffee cups out of the way and opening his laptop. It was not as if he had a choice. The screen flickered to life. The Microsoft Word document he had been working on for nearly a year was there on the screen, the cursor a thin, vertical black line of pixels blinking against a clean, glowing white, phosphorescent screen unsullied by so much as a single letter of type.

He lit one of the Camels, exhaling a tense blue plume of smoke at the screen.

Inspiration was just there, a mere thousandth of an inch beyond his grasp. Perhaps a little nicotine would coax it out of his lair and allow him, after months of anguish and procrastination, to do some honest work.

Wheeler smoked.

Wheeler stared at the computer screen.

Wheeler stubbed out the butt and lit another.

In the middle of his third cigarette, feeling a brief flicker of an idea, he raised his hands over the keyboard, only to shake his head and drop his hands back into his lap.

After forty-five minutes of sitting there, smoking and staring at the screen, Wheeler pushed back his chair and stood, ignoring the blinking red Devil's eye across the room as he went out onto the balcony. It was getting dark and starting to rain. Fifteen stories below, cars and taxis had turned on their lights against the dusk.

He put one hand on the railing and looked down. It wasn't the first time he considered throwing himself over. It wasn't even the hundredth. This was the place he ended up at the end of each failed attempt to work, looking down at the street far below, filled with feelings of impotence, despair and self-loathing.

He was too much of a coward to kill himself. And besides, he hated himself with so much passion that he would be giving himself a reward he didn't deserve by jumping to his death and putting an end to his miserable life. He deserved to suffer.

There was only one solution, the same one Wheeler had turned to a dozen other times when he got to the point of complete desperation. But first he had to be sure. He went back inside and stood staring at the answering machine. As much agony as it would add to the poisoned well of his soul, he needed to hear it. It was the final step in the terrible ritual he had gone through ever since signing his first contract.

Wheeler's nicotine-stained forefinger stabbed the play button.

"Hey there, hot shot, this is Daniel—just checking in to see how the new book is coming along. I was looking at my date book this morning, and I saw that, according to your contract, I should have had your new manuscript two months ago. There's no hurry, of course, but please call me as soon as possible—today if you can—and update me on your progress. I'm sure it's going to be another masterpiece. I can't wait to see the manuscript. Please call at your earliest convenience."

"Fuck," Wheeler said. That was what he always said when this happened. "Fuck, fuck, fuck."

He went into the kitchen, opened the drawer where he kept the corkscrew, potato peeler and other kitchen utensils and started digging around with one hand, pushing the odds-and-ends back and forth. What a damned mess, he thought; how could one drawer be such a frigging disaster?

A chilling thought grabbed Wheeler, like a hook slicing into the base of his skull: What if he couldn't find it this time? What if it was lost? The whole sacred tradition would be broken, and then what would become of him?

He could hardly remember how it had all started. He'd been practically insane when the time came for him to turn in his first book more than a decade earlier. The pressure had built up inside him, a little more with every day that passed without him being able to write, until finally, stumbling around the apartment in a nearly catatonic fugue state from the accumulated stress, he'd hit upon the perfect solution to his writer's block.

Wheeler began to haul handfuls of things out of the drawer, flinging them down on the counter and floor, frantic now to find it.

"Ah!"

An almost sexual pleasure trilled through him at the sight of the old ice pick—long silver needle of a blade and battered wooden handle—nestled at the very back of the beige plastic tray that lined the drawer.

"That was very naughty of you," he said.

Wheeler bent over, pulled up the right pant leg of his blue jeans, and slid the ice pick down his sock, smoothing the denim over it so no one would notice it.

Wheeler went to the closet where he kept his jacket and umbrella.

He was going out.

It was raining when Wheeler walked down the rusty fire escape into the unlit brick alleyway. The rain was writer's rain; the kind you get in suspense novels—dark, cold and forbidding.

His mind kept returning to his writer's block. He read dozens of articles and books about the subject—pure drivel by hackneyed wordsmiths, all trying to make a quick buck in a trade publication.

That was also the reason he didn't attend literary conventions anymore. He went to a con a couple of years ago in the godforsaken city of Cleveland. Wheeler met a New York Times best-selling author who claimed he never had writer's block in his entire career.

The man was lying straight to his face.

All writers get writer's block, like all athletes get sweaty socks.

Wheeler felt like a woolly mammoth stuck in a tar pit of literacy, struggling to get free . . . all the while sinking to the bottom too quickly.

It was the realism that made writing so hard these days. All the bestsellers had a reality edge or some bona fide insight that made their books believable. Robin Cook, a former doctor, wrote medical thrillers, John Grisham, a former lawyer, wrote legal thrillers, Father Andrew Greeley, a former priest, wrote steamy sexy religious books. Hell, it was easy being a doctor or lawyer or priest writing books about your former occupation. Try being a former librarian writing murder mysteries. The homicides had to be factual. The American public wanted authentic blood on their hands—or on the bookshelves.

All he had to do is find someone to murder. It would give him the realism he needed and he'd become unblocked. The bricks blocking him would crumble to dust and he'd have another finished novel.

A rat ran in front of him, hissing.

He pulled the ice pick out of his sock and drove it straight through the middle of the brown furry rodent, killing it instantly.

This is good, he thought as he was scraping the dead creature against a brick wall to free his ice pick. Murdering a rat is a good way to start a manuscript. Wheeler bet that Michael Crichton didn't go out slaying rodents for his novels. This was going to give him an edge. He needed more bloodletting for his book, more sacrifices for the word-gods.

He also needed a smoke. He lit up the last of his Camels. It felt good to have the warm smoke in his lungs on this chilly evening. Wheeler had walked down the trash-strewn alley for some time now, and had passed the corner of 42nd and 47th.

He stopped in front of a red brick building. It was an old apartment complex that had been a cheap hotel during the 1950s and 1960s. Wheeler peered into the window on the bottom floor. He could see through the worn curtains. He saw an old lady wearing a light blue nightgown—from a distance, she resembled his Aunt Polly, the same bun-style gray hair, the same thick reading glasses. The elderly woman was reading a Tom Clancy book. He hated Clancy with a passion. Wheeler hated Clancy even more than he hated Michael Crichton. He hated the million dollar advances, top of the best seller list every time, his novels adapted into blockbuster movies—Wheeler bet that the best selling list author didn't have to stalk victims in the night because he was two months overdue for his book and hadn't written a single goddamn page.

The ancient entity rearranged its feeding aperture in the manner representing displeasure on the human face.

Sensory deprivation had been the hardest thing it had to endure during the centuries it had been cast into outer darkness. In place of the myriad delights it had known during its earthly incarnations, there was only the black, cold nothingness of the abyss in which it drifted. If not for its memories, the entity would have gone mad—although by mortal standards the malevolent spirit had been insane since Creation's dawning. At the hollow center of the demon's soul there was only a howling savagery that blood, violence, and mortal souls could fuel but never satisfy.

Still, the demon was a being of discrimination and taste. When last in the world, it had developed a passion for the light, ethereal poetry of the Japanese imperial court. And though it might seem surprising to some that a demon could form a sentimental attachment for poems about cherry blossoms and moonlight, in the incomprehensibly vast expanse of time stretching between today and the Beginning, far stranger things had happened.

The demon turned the page and read a few more paragraphs, sighing at frequent intervals.

The prose style was plodding and lacked imagery and subtlety. The chance to read anything after so long, at first, had been bliss itself, but this particular bliss was fast becoming stale.

The demon was perplexed by the story about the Russian submarine, not knowing what either a Russian or a submarine was. Evidently human society had regressed in terms of the Russians—obvious barbarians—while progressing in terms of technology . . . not that demons had much interest in mortal progress.

The old woman whose husk the demon had taken had deplorable tastes in literature, her bookshelves filled with paperback thrillers and novels about vampires. She did possess one rare volume, an old book of incantations left behind by the previous tenant when he'd committed suicide. Roberta Pirandello had been reading out loud to herself from the chapter on summoning demons from the outer darkness when she got what was both the biggest and final surprise of her wretchedly dull life. Roberta belonged to the demon now, body and soul, her mortal form the means by which the entity could experience the sensations earthly life had to offer.

It was not a body the entity much appreciated. It was old and creaky and not the least bit attractive to demons, who appreciate physical beauty the same as anybody else. But it would do for now, until something better came along. And so the demon sat and read, pleasuring itself sexually with the fingers of its free hand, waiting for an opportunity to do evil to come along, as it always did.

There was a noise, the hush of breath against the windowpane, and the demon began to smile, knowing, the way a spider knows when a soft vibration in the air signals the approach of an insect toward its web, that a delicious opportunity is being born.

Keeping its head tilted forward and the left eye moving across the pages open on its lap, the demon rotated the right eye upward to peer surreptitiously through the loose tendrils of gray hair, at the voyeur peeking in through the window.

Wheeler sat at his desk typing with a maddening fury, his fingers stabbing the keyboard without mercy. He completed the manuscript in record time. Free of his writer's block, he wrote like a man possessed, not sleeping for the six days it took him to finish the new novel in one furious, brilliant draft.

He went into the cupboard, opened the door and took out a bottle of one-hundred year old Scotch he always drank from after he finished a book. It tasted sweeter than true love. He pushed the cork back in, sidling toward the table where his laptop waited, still on.

Wheeler could feel it burning in his soul: the idea for another novel. He would slam out a proposal for the new book to send along with the manuscript, the same as he always did.

Now that he was hitting his stride, he would be able to write more than one book a year. Since he no longer needed to sleep, he could write a book a week — maybe more, if the ice pick found him the right inspiration.

The writer picked up his bloodstained ice pick from where it sat next to his printer. He lifted the hand tool to his mouth and ran his tongue along the blade, tasting the old woman's dried blood, smiling at the iron-rich taste.

They say writers are driven by a need to exorcise their inner demons.

For Wheeler, the line dividing the demon from the writer had ceased to exist.

Mike: *I work well with Mark McLaughlin. That's the reason we write together so much. Most of our stories involve a lot of laughs. That was especially true for "The Ten Klown-Mandments." I remember a week of belly laughs, each of us coming up with funnier and funnier material. This story first appeared in Delirium Magazine. The story started with a funny premise—Moses as a killer clown—and just kept getting sillier, darker and more outrageous until the turbo-charged conclusion.*

Mark: *This story may be filled with blasphemy, but it was certainly a blast for me, writing it with Mike! I think this is my favorite collaboration with Mike, because the main character is so gleefully wicked. I've always loved villains more than heroes. They're so much more memorable. Think of the classic Universal monster movies, featuring Dracula, the Mummy, Frankenstein's Monster, the Wolf Man and Gill Man. Can you remember the names of the good guys? You may have remembered Van Helsing easily enough, but I bet you had trouble recalling the rest!*

THE TEN KLOWN-MANDMENTS

Mark McLaughlin & Michael McCarty

Klowny wasn't always a kult klown.

He started out as a healthy, perfectly kute baby. His mommy even stopped drinking and whoring long enough to karry and deliver him. But a kouple weeks after he squirmed his way out of her, mommy went out boozing with some of the other strippers from the bar where she worked. She didn't want to spring for a babysitter, so she plunked little Karl Lawrence Downy—that was his name back then—into the big kitchen wastebasket. That way if he took a poop, she'd only have to rinse him off. When she got back around two a.m., Karl was screaming his lungs out just because a rat was nibbling on his face. What a krybaby!

Mommy took one look at Karl's chewed-up face and decided that motherhood wasn't in the kards for her. So she popped the kid into a jumbo fried-chicken bucket, tossed in a baby picture taken by one of the hospital volunteers—no sense having an unpleasant reminder like that lying around—and threw him out the window.

But luck was on Karl's side. Fifteen minutes earlier, a psychopath had tossed the kut-up chunks of a hooker down a manhole, and he'd neglected to shut the lid behind her. The chicken bucket flew down the hole, right into the sewer.

The bucket flowed through the soupy darkness, down a forgotten passageway of shit and despair. And the hooker's head floated right beside it. Eventually the sewer led out to the river, and Karl blinked sleepily in the moonlight. He looked over the edge of the bucket and saw the deadhead—she looked so nice with her lavender eyeshadow and pink blush and kandy-red lipstick. So pretty!

Suddenly a big cheery voice sang out, "What do we have here?" A bamboo kane snagged the bucket and drew it to the edge of the river. Then white-gloved hands picked up the baby.

Mazey-Belle, Kween of the Big-Top, took a long look at Karl and pouted. "You poor bastard," she whispered. She pulled a stream of knotted, multi-kolored hankies out of her sleeve. She wiped the blood and filth off him with the first one, and then wrapped the rest of the hankies around him like a blanket.

She took him to her tent in the circus kamp. Her husband, King Komedy, gasped when he saw what she was karrying. "Where'd you find that sad little kritter?"

Mazey-Belle flashed him a gap-toothed smile. "The Lord gave him to me. It's a miracle. After all these long years, a miracle."

"He's sure torn-up," King said.

"Then it's a good thing the Lord gave us make-up." She studied her new son's ravaged face. "And rubber noses and wigs. Don't you see? He was *meant* to be a klown."

"Hey, what's this stuck to his ass?" Her husband peeled the soggy baby picture off the kid's bottom. He squinted at the name printed in kapital letters on the back. Initials and a last name: the ink was smeared, so the first two letters of the last name had run together. "K...L...OWNY...? Mazey-Belle, it really *is* a miracle! His name is KLOWNY! Why, that's perfect! He'll be our little Prince of Klowns! He won't ever want to be no doctor or lawyer if he knows he was born to wear greasepaint." He looked at the little face and shuddered. "Besides, nobody in their right mind would want a doctor with a kisser like that."

Klowny joined the act as soon as he learned to walk. By age five, he'd learned to juggle, walk the tightrope, and even swallow little swords. Mazey-Belle did his make-up when he woke up in the morning, refreshed it during the day, and washed it off with his evening bath, just before he went to bed. He grew up thinking of the make-up as his real face, and didn't even realize that he might look a little different without it.

But eventually there kame a morning when Klowny wanted to put on his make-up by himself.

"Oh, but I have so much fun doing it," Mazey-Belle said.

"Now, honey," King said. "The boy will have to put on his own make-up eventually." He opened a drawer in his nightstand and pulled out a mirror. "Look at this, boy. Tell me what you see."

Klowny took the mirror and gazed at his reflection. "Oh." For a full minute he was silent. Then he said, "What are all those funny lines? Other people don't got 'em."

"Those are kalled scars, son," King said. "You know you've got enough make-up on when you kan't see them any more."

"And how kome some of my nose is missing?"

"That's so your nice red-rubber one will fit more snugly over it," The old man stated, smiling.

"You were meant to be a klown! The best ever!" Mazey-Belle brought out all the tubes and jars and kans of make-up. "Always remember, son! For a klown, every day is *showtime!*"

In the years that followed, ticket sales for the circus began to drop. People were too interested in the internet to bother leaving their homes for entertainment. The world seemed to be turning into one big office. Eventually the circus fired the klown family.

They took their savings and rented a little apartment in a big metro area. They began looking for work. To make ends meet, they entertained at kids' birthday parties every now and then.

One day King kame home with some news. "I've found steady work for all of us!" he said. "From now on, we're going to be korporate klowns!"

"I don't even know what that means!" Mazey-Belle said.

"For PharaohPlex!" He held out a sheet of letterhead with a golden pyramid logo. "It's a multinational konglomerate, run by billionaire Lazlo Goldencalf. PharaohPlex has hundreds of thousands of busy workers, and we're going to join their stress-relief program, klowning around at all their offices to keep the troops entertained."

"That sounds terrific," the klown-kween said.

"Troops? You mean slaves!" Klowny said. "Sorry, mom and dad, but you're going to have to do it without me!"

The parents were shocked. "But why?" King asked.

"Because korporations are no fun!" the son said. "Office-slaves may need entertaining, but I'm not the klown for the job." So saying, he rushed off to his room. Ten minutes later he kame back out with a bandanna-wrapped bundle on the end of a big stick. "It's time for me to hit the road. There's a world of fun out there, and I'm gonna get me a slice!" A moment later a door slam echoed through the apartment.

Klowny tried his best to get a good old-fashioned klown job, but there just weren't any left.

He made balloon animals for the kids in restaurants and did a few kommercials for small-town TV stations, but that wasn't enough to make a living.

A klown has to eat, so eventually he was reduced to doing klown-porn. He told himself it was just a giggle, all in fun. He started out with a bit-part in *Honk If You're Horny*. Within just three months, he had starring roles in *Rubber Chicken Mama* and *Face In Your Pie*. Pretty soon he got kaught up in the lifestyle: nonstop parties, orgies, and eventually, designer klown drugs—Jollies and Fi-Fi's and Happy Dust. And Happy Dust made Klowny very happy indeed.

The problem was, too much Dust kan take the bounce out of a klown's pogo stick. And the stuff was expensive. With no work in sight, Klowny decided to relieve PharaohPlex of some of its kash—surely a multinational konglomerate wouldn't miss a few bucks!

PharaohPlex owned a chain of shopping centers kalled Red C Superstores. Klowny recruited a dozen tough kids from an inner-city playground and led them into the store, laughing and playing. The klerks gave him strange looks, but what kould they do? Who kan protest a klown showing a bunch of poor kids a good time? Soon all the shoppers were laughing at Klowny's antics. Even the security guards were kracking up—until the kids took the bricks from their backpacks and kracked up the jewelry displays.

Klowny tossed smoke bombs at the guards and then snatched up the shiniest goodies in the broken displays. The kids did some snatching, too, and soon the klown and his kohorts were scurrying out the front doors, still laughing their asses off.

In time, the kids grew older and Klowny's krimes grew bolder. And always, they were aimed at the PharaohPlex family of stores, factories, research labs and kredit unions.

Along the way, a few guards here and there had to die. Some police officers, too. But Klowny had developed a philosophy: if you're not making the world a fun place, then you deserve to die. Or, to put it simply—kill the killjoys!

His posse eventually decided to wear klown klothes just like their leader, and each took on a new komic persona. His most dedicated followers were Rat-Butt, who wore whiskers and a scaly tail in addition to his tramp-klown klothes, and Kitty-Boo, who looked like a kross between a tabby and a harlequin. The two of them had the kraziest fights! Klowny was proud of his new family of kartoon kut-ups, so he introduced them to the delicious mysteries of Happy Dust.

Klowny found he had a flair for inventing. So, he developed a deadly arsenal of klown krime weapons and krazy kontraptions: exploding balloon animals . . . kream pies made with flesh-eating bacteria . . . even pogo sticks with flame-throwers and machine guns mounted on the handles.

Of kourse, all those inventions took a back seat to the greatest wonder of them all. Once, after a few fine hits of Happy Dust, Klowny prayed to the oldest Klown of all, whose nose was as red as the pit of Hell. The Great Klown was pleased with His disciple's progress, so He granted Klowny a vision, showing him how to tweak a few scientific principles here and there.

That was the day Klowny and his kohorts kombined three komputers, a microwave oven, some quartz krystals and a shrimpy little kar to kreate a scientific marvel—the Klownmobile.

The doors of this rainbow-striped kompact opened into a larger, self-kontained pocket of the space/time kontinuum, so it seated thirteen klowns easily. Once everyone was inside, Klowny would hit the IMPLODE button to make the outside of the Klownmobile become as wee as a toy-kar, while the inside stayed the same komfortable size.

"Klowny, this kar is the tom-kat's testicles," said Kitty-Boo. "So what are we gonna steal first with it? The Mona Lisa? Gold from Fort Knox? The treasures of the Vatican?"

"Let's steal cheese!" Rat-Butt said. "We're fresh out! I just finished off the last of the Limburger!"

Irritated, the kat klown gave Rat-Butt a scratch across his long bent nose. The rodent retaliated by firing a fetid belch at the feline felon, kausing him to faint.

"My friends," Klowny said, "believe it or not, we are going to steal *kriminals!*"

From that point on, Klowny would allow himself to be arrested and incarcerated every few months. Kriminals, after all, were just happy folks who had too much fun for other people's liking. With each visit to the pen, Klowny would build a power base of devoted followers. Then, Rat-Butt or Kitty-Boo would drive the shrunken Klownmobile into the prison yard—enlarge it just long enough to let Klowny hop in, along with whatever kriminals he'd taken a liking to—and then shrink back down and drive off.

Klowny was kollecting the best of the worst—master thieves, exotic perverts, serial killers and a wild assortment of lunatics and human oddities. The growing posse took over a forgotten trailer kourt in a valley a few miles from a mountain range. There they began building lopsided, gaudy homes. In their new kommunity, they worshipped the power and glory that was the Great Klown. That was the beginning of KlownTown and the Church of the Red Rubber Nose.

Growing in rural seclusion, KlownTown eventually became more like a city. The enormous Church of the Red Rubber Nose towered over all of the town's multi-kolored, ramshackle buildings. The krazy kathedral was made of dozens of trailers piled and welded together into a mass roughly shaped like the human figure. This the builders had painted black; they'd then draped the figure in sheets of tin, bent, kurled and painted to resemble a frilly-kollared shirt and baggy pants.

The pleasure-seeking excesses of the Townies rivalled those of Kaligula and De Sade. Their favorite diversion was abducting substitute teachers—killjoys like that would not be missed. The Townies built huge mazes out of boards studded with rusty nails and barbed wire. They would then throw the teachers into the mazes and release the robotic rubber chickens, which had razorblade beaks and klaws.

The Townies folowed that by throwing an all-afternoon barbecue, roasting the chunks and shreds left by the robo-chickens.

It took the authorities years to locate KlownTown. Once they found it, what did they do to dismantle the krime kommunity...?

Nothing.

Kounty government kowered in the shadows.

State government pocketed bribes and looked the other way.

National government mired the issue in red tape. The town

was also inhabited by klown strippers and hookers, many of whom had children. They kouldn't just storm in with bazookas and army tanks. Especially since the klowns *also* had bazookas and army tanks.

Only one force on Earth was big enough to deal with KlownTown.

That force was PharaohPlex.

Klowny looked up at a pair of golden PharaohPlex helicopters whirling above KlownTown.

"Well, well, well," Klowny said. "Mosquito season already! Get out the swatters, boys!"

Ratt-Butt and Kitty-Boo loaded two huge kannons and fired. Thick signposts with flags that said BANG!!! poked out of the cylinders. Then the klowns pressed little red buttons on the kannons and the signposts shot like rockets into the air, each spearing a helicopter and exploding — for the hollow posts were filled with nitroglycerin.

A tiny serial killer named Gned the Gnat ran up to Klowny. "Boss!" he kried, "some PharaohPlex bulldozers are heading this way!"

"Oh, we've got enough dynamite to take kare of a few measly bulldozers," the top klown said.

"Would you kall two-hundred 'a few'?" Gned said.

"Great sizzling sausages!" Klowny kried. "Time to break out the Klown Kurses!"

"Not the Klown Kurses . . . " Gned whispered in awe.

"You bet your boner! It's time to open a jumbo-sized kan of whoop-tooshy on those korporate kreeps!" Klowny gestured for Rat-Butt and Kitty-Boo to follow him, and the three key klowns headed for the kathedral.

Around the sides of the Church of the Red Rubber Nose stood ten black storage sheds. Klowny took a big black key out of his vest pocket and opened the padlock on one of the doors.

Venomous South American tree-frogs, purple and yellow and orange and red, kame hopping out of the first shed. Klowny pointed in the direction of the bulldozers. "Go get 'em, my pretties!" he screamed, and the kritters went hopping off. As he opened the rest of the sheds, he sang a little song:

"Froggies hop and batsies fly—
dozer drivers soon will die!
Boils from wasps and bites from rats,
scratches from some beastly kats!
Monkeys shooting squirt-guns filled
with blood from stiffs a plague has killed!
On my foes shall locusts gnaw!
Klowny starts to laugh—guffaw!
Here a robot that shows scorn
to any driver who's first-born:
those poor jerks will find their butts
sliced up into some fresh kold-kuts.
Ravens love to peck out eyes—
so try some darkness on for size!"

Klowny was so happy, he skipped behind the kathedral to his private shit-shed, a bright-orange outhouse, to take a kongratulatory dump. Then he and his two klown korporals klimbed the stairs to the top of the kathedral and watched from a high window as the Klown Kurses descended upon the bull-dozers. The other citizens of KlownTown klimbed on top of their dwellings to observe the karnage, too.

Gned the Gnat joined Klowny on the kathedral observation deck. "We've kaptured one of the drivers. He said that PharaohPlex is building a new city—along with a factory and a shopping center—at the base of Mt. Rumba, about thirty miles from here."

Klowny nodded. "Fetch the pogo-umbrellas, the seltzer bottles and some explosives. It's klear we've won this battle—those drivers don't stand a chance. Now it's time for some of us to pay a little visit to their konstruction site."

A few minutes later, Klowny and his original dirty dozen were gathered by the enormous kannons. The klowns were loaded into the big guns and fired toward the konstruction area. Once they were airborne, they pulled out the seltzer bottles and started spritzing. The seltzer was a special high-power mix, and it sent them flying on for miles. When they were over the building site, they dropped their bottles and opened the pogo-umbrellas. They all settled gently to the ground, right in front of a brand-new Red C Superstore.

Klowny smiled. "Okay, let's plant the explosives," he said, klosing his umbrella. The others also klosed theirs. He happened to glance up toward Mt. Rumba. Then something kaught his eye. "Hey, what's that burning way up there...?"

"First things first, Boss!" Rat-Butt said. "Look over by that factory—security guards are heading this way!"

Klowny ignored him and stared up at the swirl of flames high up on the mountain. So red—as red as his Master's nose . . . "We're gonna check out that fire, boys—but this krappy store is in the way!" He raised his pogo-umbrella. "By the Power of the Great Klown, I kommand this Red C to part and allow us passage!"

The earth shook and thundered, toppling klowns and security guards alike. Only Klowny remained standing, holding his arms out wide. With a resounding *krack!* the huge building split down the middle, and the two halves each slid to the side. "On your sticks, boys! It's time to roll!"

The klowns quickly unfolded the handles and footpedals of their pogo-umbrellas. They then began to hop along on their klown kontraptions right through the split Red C toward Mt. Rumba.

A moment later, the security guards were back on their feet, chasing them. By that time, Klowny and his posse were on the other side of the broken building.

Klowny turned and raised his pogo-umbrella again. "Time to klose up shop!"

With a sudden *smack!* the two halves lunged back together, katching the guards in the middle. Klowny whisked his gloves together like a housewife shaking flour off her hands.

"Hey, Boss," Kitty-Boo said. "We've got kompany."

Klowny turned around. Before him stood a tall, distinguished man in a white business suit, along with two elderly klowns.

"Hello, Klowny," the tall man said. He smiled. "Nice of you to put my store back together."

Klowny raised a bright red eyebrow. "I don't believe we've been introduced."

"Well, I believe you already know your parents . . . " The tall man gestured toward the klown kouple. "I am Lazlo Goldencalf, CEO of PharaohPlex." He held out his hand. "Mazey-Belle and King Komedy have told me so much about you. They love you, Klowny. I think that deep down, you're a great guy who might still have a bright future."

"Shake the man's hand and say you're sorry, son!" Mazey-Belle said. "This krime spree of yours has got to stop! Lazlo is a good man! His kompany gives jobs to lots of grateful folks worldwide!"

"Do the right thing, my boy!" King Komedy implored. "It's not too late to rehabilitate you and your gang. Lazlo has said that he'll even pay for the therapy!"

"Horse nuggets!" Klowny kried. "My boys and me ain't gonna become a bunch of slave-robots in suits! Plus, this old kreep sent a bunch of bulldozers to flatten us!"

Lazlo gasped. "They weren't going to kill you! They were going to smooth the land around your kommunity so we kould start building you a *proper* town!"

"Yeah? And what about those security guards we just kreamed?" Klowny said.

"Security forces are instructed to greet newcomers and give them a guided tour!" Tears rolled down the old man's face. "They didn't even have guns!"

Rat-Butt hitched a thumb toward the CEO and the senior klowns. "I say we turn these three into Swiss cheese!" He pulled a miniature machine gun out of one of the pockets of his baggy tramp pants.

Lazlo shook his head sadly. "All I've ever wanted to do is make the world safe, efficient and productive. I've always felt that I kould trust my fellow man. Kould it be that I've been wrong?"

"That's right, old man—but cheer up! You may be a moron, but you'll make an excellent hostage!" Klowny turned toward his gang. "Tie up these three bozos and send a ransom note. Then bring the rest of the klowns here and set up kamp. Oh, and bring my shit-shed from behind the kathedral. That's my favorite krapper!" He looked up at the fire on the mountain—he kould feel a wave of exhiliration stirring within his soul. "I'm going there alone, but I'll be koming down soon with a big heapin' slop-bucket of *destiny!*"

Klowny skipped up the mountain trail. Now that he had that goody-two-shoes Lazlo in his klutches, he figured it would be easy to deprogram his befuddled, brainwashed parents.

Even now and then he stopped to eat some berries or grapes or big, tasty grubs he found along the trail. The fruit made him a little queasy, but the bugs settled his stomach. He'd get some real food when he returned to kamp—he'd make a big fried-chicken, bacon and mint ice-kream sundae, smothered in tabasco sauce.

Soon he found himself approaching the red swirl of fire. It was, in fact, a huge, blazing . . . office plant.

A Flaming Fern.

It spoke to him in a happy, musical tone. "Welcome to the KlownZone. What's shakin'?"

"Wow, I wish I'd known this place was so klose to KlownTown! I'd have stopped by sooner," Klowny said.

Some of the leaves kurled into a smile. "This is just a temporary location. In fact, we're here just to meet you!"

"In that kase," he said, "I'd like to have a chat with the big guy."

"Sure—it'll be a minute, though. He's on the trans-dimensional kommunicator right now." The plant unfurled a long leaf his way, revealing a dish of white powder. "Here's some Happy Dust to take the edge off your wait."

"That's mighty neighborly of ya," Klowny said.

"No problem. It's like the Boss says—'If you're not having fun, what's the point?'"

Klowny took the dish and snuffed Happy Dust up each nostril, rubbed some on his teeth, and then put some in his ears and a little up his butt, too. By the time the Great Klown was ready to see him, he was flying high.

The Fern pointed toward a entryway made of huge chunks of basalt. Klowny passed through and found himself in an enormous toychest, filled with giant teddybears and dollies and playtime soldiers.

In the center of the chest stood a giant jack-in-the-box with purple and orange klown silhouettes painted on the sides. The giant toy began to play a strident war march. Then the lid sprang open, and a bloated, star-spangled spider-klown popped out, bobbing up and down on its rusty spring. Its only feature that was even vaguely human was its shiny red rubber nose. Its six eyes glowed red and green and yellow. Globules of teal venom spooled down from its barbed fangs.

The spider-klown waved its front legs in the air. Rat-Butt and Kitty-Boo materialized in the air, their arms and legs thrashing madly.

"Hey, what do you want with those two?" Klowny said.

"*Need . . .* " The voice of the Great Klown was like the thick, plopping purr of bubbling tar. "*Something . . . to . . . write on . . .* "

The next morning, Klowny appeared on a ridge overlooking the new Klown Kamp at the base of Mt. Rumba. He held in his arms two ragged skins, each etched with bloody sacred words.

"Listen up, you klowns!" he screamed. The people below began to kongregate at the foot of the ridge. "I've got some Dead Klown Skrolls here, and they kontain some important information. The Great Klown Himself took the time from His busy eternity to write down the rules of how you chuckleheads should live—so listen up, 'kuz these are the Ten Klown-Mandments!"

Klowny kleared his throat, held up the skrolls and began to sing:

"Don't dis the Klown, 'kuz if you do,
He'll turn you into sticky goo!

The Klown's yer daddy! Them's the facts—
know your place or get the axe!

Put no other before the Klown:
He's the King of dark renown!

Get a piece! It's loads of fun—
Klowny loves to shoot his gun . . .

And if the Klown forgets to kall,
chill out or you'll take a fall!

Go ahead and steal all day—
Every Klown needs toys for play!

Your ass is mine, and so's your mule—
give 'em here, don't be a fool.

But still, each Klown's one of a kind!
Kopykats a grave will find!

Every day's a circus, buddy!
Have some fun or end up bloody!

Thou shalt kill in komedy!
A boring life is BLASPHEMY!"

Once he was finished, Klowny looked out over the masses.
They were standing in neat rows, all holding hands.

In the center of the front row stood Lazlo Goldencalf. On
each side of him stood his parents and the remainder of his
posse.

"Great glistening gargoyle gonads!" Klowny wailed. "What's

going on here? I go off for two seconds and all heaven breaks loose!"

Gned the Gnat, who was riding on Lazlo's shoulders, hung his head. "What kan we say, Boss? This guy's got deep pockets—deeper than any klown's. He gave us all great jobs with the korporation. We're on his payroll now."

Lazlo raised his shining eyes to Klowny. "There is work for you to do, too, my son. Just say the word."

Klowny sneered. "I'll do better than that! I have *three* words for all of you: KISS…MY…ASS!"

So saying, he ripped the skrolls to shreds and kame storming down off the ridge.

"I kan't believe it! I knock myself out, trying to kreate a world of wild, reckless fun for you goofballs, and what do you do? You go and get *respectable* on me! Well, doesn't that just take the koconut kream pie!"

He marched right up to his private shit-shed. "Well, gang," he said. "It was fun while it lasted, but frankly, now you washed-up wussy wimps make me wanna puke up everything I've ever eaten in my whole life. It's a good thing I had a back-up plan, just in kase this kind of hog-feces ever hit the fan! So long, you miserable kluster of kanker-sores—'kuz I'm outta here!"

He stepped into the krapper and klosed the door. For a moment, there was silence. Then, two aerodynamic fins sprang out on either side of the little building. The roof opened up and refolded itself into a nose-kone. As the krowd watched, the shit-shed transformed into a sleek shit-ship.

"Where kan he go in such a small rocket?" Lazlo whispered.

"It's small on the *outside*," Gned said, "but Klowny knows how to make his vehicles big on the *inside*. It kould be as big as a palace in there."

The shit-ship began to sputter—then chug—then it rumbled to demonic life. A flaming radioactive heat-blast poured out of vents in the base of the ship as it rose into the air. It circled several times over Lazlo and his new krew of korporate klowns, reducing them all to glowing ashes.

Klowny then shifted into mega-ultra-hyperdrive, and his bright-orange shit-ship soared off into space, in search of a little kosmic fun.

Because every day is showtime.

CODA: ABOUT THE AUTHORS

P.D. CACEK:

The author of over two hundred short stories, three novels and a collection, P.D. Cacek has won both a World Fantasy and Bram Stoker Award. She is wrote the novels *Night Prayer, Night Players* (Design Image), *Canyons* (Tor) and the chapbook *In The Spirit* (Wormhole Books). She is currently working on the second book of what she's calling her New Hope Quartet—a series of non-traditional gothic ghost stores set in New Hope, Pennsylvania. Cacek currently lives in Doylestown, PA.—only a few miles from her beloved New Hope, as the bat flies. Her website is http://www.pdcacek.com

SANDRA DELUCA:

Sandra Deluca's fiction and poetry appeared in such places as "Space And Time," "The Edge," "Darkness Within," "Divas Of Darkness," "The Thorns Of Nature," "October Rush" and "The Urbanite." Her poetry chapbook *Burial Plot In Sagittarius* was nominated for a Bram Stoker award in 2000. Her latest publication is a collection of short stories and poems from Double Dragon Publishing called *Paths Of Destiny*. She recently completed a short novel called *Settling In Nazareth,* a crime noir book with supernatural elements. When not creating her own fiction, poetry or artwork, she pursues her hobbies, which include photography, researching old myths, legends and religions. For more information on this diverse talented author and artist, visit Sandy DeLuca on the web at http://www.decembergirlpress.com

CRISTOPHER HENNESSEY-DEROSE:

Following jaunts into amateur soccer and way too many rock bands in the '80s, Cristopher Hennessey-DeRose found his start writing genre fiction and has had about hundred pieces appear in publication like "Gothic.Net" and "Talesbones." His novellas *The Pale* and *The Adagio Chronicles* have been published by Black Cat Press and Graveworm Press, respectively. His novel, *Lives Of Future Past*, was published by Black Cat Press.

R.L. FOX:

He was born in Iowa, but that hasn't stopped him from seeing the rest of the world, including Panama, Columbia, Saudi Arabia, Italy and even Iraq (served in Desert Storm). His fiction and poetry has appeared in such magazines as "Frightmares," "The Reaper" and "Goddess Of The Bay."

CINDY HULTING:

A former beauty queen and CIA agent, Cindy Hulting's bio is classified information and wasn't available through the Freedom of Information Act.

CHARLEE JACOB:

Charlee Jacob's Stoker-nominated novella *Dread In The Beast* is now a novel, out soon from Necro Publications with an introduction by Edward Lee. In addition, Delirium Books is publishing her novel, *Vestal*. DNA Publications is publishing her dark fantasy novel *Dark Moods* and a collection of vampire fiction and poetry called *The Indigo People*. She is the author of *This Symbiotic Fascination* (Necro and Leisure Books) and *Haunter* (Leisure) as well as several fiction collections and poetry chapbooks. She is fifty-one and lives in Irving, Texas, with her husband, Jim.

TERI JACOBS:

Teri A. Jacobs is the author *The Void* (Leisure Books) and the forthcoming *Secrets Of The Bones* (Catalyst Press, limited hardcover edition). Her short fiction has appeared in numerous places such as "Flesh & Blood Magazine," "Gothic.Net," "Horror Garage," Dark Testament, and Decadence 1 & 2. At the moment, Teri wears the hats of assistant editor for "Flesh & Blood Magazine" and fiction/poetry editor of "The Horror Within," and is at work on her next novel, *Carnevale*. So saith Thomas Ligotti of *The Void*: "Teri A. Jacobs ambitiously and relentlessly pursues a darkness beyond darkness . . . "

BENTLEY LITTLE:

Born in Arizona shortly after his mother attended the world premiere of *Psycho*, Bentley Little attended California State University at Fullerton, where he earned a B.A. in communications and an M.A. in English and comparative literature. He has worked as a technical writer, reporter/photographer, library assistant, sales clerk, phonebook deliveryman, video arcade attendant, newspaper deliveryman, furniture mover, window washer and rodeo gatekeeper. The son of a Russian artist and an American educator, he and his Chinese wife were married by the justice of the peace in Tombstone, Arizona. They have one son. Bentley Little is the author of the Bram Stoker Award-winning novel *The Revelation*, *The Mailman*, *Death Instinct* (under the pseudonym "Phillip Emmons"), *The Summoning*, *University*, *Dominion*, *The Ignored*, *The Store*, *The House*, *The Town*, *The Walking*, *The Association*, *The Collection*, *The Return* and *The Policy*.

MICHAEL MCCARTY:

Michael McCarty is a former stand-up comedian, musician and managing editor of a music magazine. His first book *Giants Of The Genre* (Wildside Press) is a collection of interviews with the greats of science fiction, horror, fantasy writers including Dean Koontz, Ray Bradbury, Peter Straub, Neil Gaiman, Charlee Jacob, P.D. Cacek, Bentley Little and thirteen others. His next book is the sequel *More Giants Of The Genre*, which will feature twenty-five interviews. *Dark Duets* is his first fiction collection. Michael graduated from Marycrest College with a B.A. in both English and Journalism. His website is http://www.geocities.com /mccartyzone. He can also be reached at: P.O. Box 4441, Rock Island, IL 61201, monstermike69@hotmail.com

MARK McLAUGHLIN:

Mark McLaughlin's fiction, nonfiction and poetry have appeared in more than 600 publications, including "The Black Gate," "Black October," "Galaxy," "Talebones," *The Book of Final Flesh, The Last Continent: New Tales of Zothique,* two volumes of *The Best Of The Rest,* and two volumes of *The Year's Best Horror Stories.* The most recent collections of his work include *Once Upon A Slime,* a trade paperback from Catalyst Books; *Hell Is Where The Heart Is,* 400+ pages of horror stories from Medium Rare Books; *Motivational Shriker,* a limited-edition from Delirium Books; and two chapbooks of poetry from Yellow Bat Press—*Your Handy Office Guide To Corporate Monsters* and *The Spiderweb Tree.* Mark won the Bram Stoker Award for Superior Achievement in Poetry 2002, along with Rain Graves and David Niall Wilson, for *The Gossamer Eye,* a three-author poetry paperback from Meisha Merlin Publishing. His website is http://www.geocities.com/ mcmonstrous.

MICHAEL ROMKEY:

Michael Romkey lives in Bettendorf, Iowa, near the Mississippi River. He is the author of *I, Vampire, The Vampire Papers, The Vampire Princess, The Vampire Virus, Vampire Hunter, The London Vampire Panic, The Vampire's Violin* and *Fear's Point.* His newest book, *American Gothic,* tracing the story of a vampire from the Civil War through the present, was published in 2004. For more information, visit his website, http://www.thevampire.com

JEFFREY THOMAS:

Jeffrey Thomas is the author of the novels *Letters From Hades*

(Bedlam Press), *Monstrocity* (Prime), the novella *Godhead Dying Downwards* (Earthling Publications) and the collections *Terror Incognita* (Delirium Books), *Aaaiiieee!!! The Best Horror Stories Of Jeffrey Thomas* (Writer's Club Press), and *Punktown* (Ministry Of Whimsy Press), a story from which was reprinted in *The Year's Best Fantasy And Horror #14*. Forthcoming are his novels *Boneland* (Bloodletting Press) and *Everybody Scream!* (Raw Dog Screaming Press), the erotic collection *Honey Is Sweeter Than Blood* (Delirium), and the Lovecraftian collection *Unholy Dimensions* (Mythos Books). Prime will be releasing an expanded hardcover edition of *Punktown* and a German language edition will feature cover art by H.R. Giger. His website is www.necropolitanpress.com